KIARAN

Immortal Highlander, Clan Mag Raith Book 5

HAZEL HUNTER

HH ONLINE

❦

Hazel loves hearing from readers!
You can contact her at the links below.

Website: hazelhunter.com

Facebook:
business.facebook.com/HazelHunterAuthor

Newsletter: HazelHunter.com/news

I send newsletters with details on new releases, special offers, and other bits of news related to my writing. You can sign up here!

Chapter One

A HEAVY MIST and thin gray skies greeted Kiaran mag Raith that morning as he walked out of the stronghold. Such damp, chill dawns spelled the end of summer in the Scottish highlands, or so he recalled from a time now made equally foggy. He could blame too many centuries and his general disinterest for his fading memories, but that had become a convenient excuse.

"Fair morning, Brother," Broden mag Raith greeted him as he walked out from the barn. The smile on the trapper's handsome face echoed the glowing joy in his eyes. "I'd offer to take morning patrol for you–"

"–but I will hurt him if he does," Mariena

Douet said as she joined them. Tall, slender, and strong, the pale Frenchwoman also appeared blissful. "Of course, I will feel guilty after, and heal him. Absorbing his wounds will then make me suffer, which will hurt him more, and he will–" She broke off in a laugh as Broden scooped her up and tossed her over his shoulder.

"Another time, Brother," the trapper said as he carried his lover toward the stronghold.

"Never fall in love, *mon ami*," Mariena called back to him. "It is the mess."

If there was one thing he could assure her, it was that. "Aye, my lady."

Once they entered the stronghold Kiaran didn't bother to continue feigning a smile. Appreciating or even envying the happiness Broden and his lady had found together wasn't impossible for him. It simply required more effort than he cared to make. Since coming to the ruined castle of Dun Chaill with his band of Pritani brothers, Kiaran had felt himself growing quieter, more detached, and less interested in everything. He'd also done things of which he should have felt ashamed, but truly didn't. The changes had not been entirely unexpected, but they now added to the inescapable burdens he had brought with him.

Soon, Kiaran thought as he rolled his aching shoulders, he would have to act, before he no longer cared about the consequences.

A flutter of black-spotted wings fanned his face before a small, gray-headed kestrel alighted on his shoulder. Sift chittered, his dark eyes catching the first rays of sun to turn a rich golden amber. Through the mind connection Kiaran shared with the raptor he saw a flash of his own strong features, carved stark and cold by weariness. The red-gold mane that framed them looked tangled and wild, but it was the dark blue eyes staring at him from his own thoughts that made him end the link.

He hated seeing the flat lifelessness in them.

Sift pecked at his ear and uttered a scolding sound. Hardly larger than a man's fist, the raptor had been the first male kestrel Kiaran had tamed. Sift usually wasn't the first to greet him in the morning, however, which stirred his sluggish curiosity.

"Where is your lady and the flight?" Kiaran murmured to the kestrel, who cried sharply before he flew off toward the forest.

Following the bird took less effort than reaching out with his tired mind to locate the rest of the kestrels. Using his power to see through the eyes of his raptors had become more difficult since his nights had grown sleepless and dreary. More often now when he tried, the images from the birds returned in a nonsensical jumble.

'Tisnae the lack of sleep. You're losing your power. Soon the kestrels shall fly away from you.

Kiaran shoved aside that growing fear as he made his way into the ancient forest. While his raptors meant everything to him, even that worry no longer preyed on him as it had.

At last he saw all the kestrels hovering over a small clearing with a swath of broken, wilting lilies and fern. The flowers and plants had been wrenched out of the ground by some disturbance, and lay heaped over a long narrow mound along with many slender branches from the surrounding trees.

He drew his sword as he scanned the clearing for signs of intruders. "Who comes here? Show yourself."

A low, soft moan came from the lilies, and the kestrels floated down and disappeared beneath the debris.

Quickly he waded into the ruined greenery,

halting as he saw what had fallen into the forest. "Fack me."

The female lay on her side, her long hair spilling like spun garnet across her face, shoulders and breasts. Petals from the lilies covered her as if she'd been strewn with them by an adoring lover, and their cool sweet scent enveloped her. The rose-gold tint of her skin and faint shimmering movement of her hair assured him she was alive. All around her his kestrels nestled as if trying to warm her with their small bodies. Dive, the flight's dominant female, looked up at him with something like despair in her dark eyes.

"'Twill be well. Let me see to her," Kiaran said. He sheathed his blade and knelt down as he gently turned her onto her back, scattering the birds.

Her young, strong body had not a mark on it, and appeared to be as well-nourished and cosseted as that of a noble woman. She wore nothing but a thin loop of frayed leather with a gleaming pendant around her throat. Looking over her torso and limbs to check for injuries, of which he saw none, he pulled off his tartan and covered her with it. Only then did he brush the hair back from her mouth and eyes.

She might have the body of a queen, but she had the face of a goddess.

Kiaran slowly took his hand away from her, but he couldn't stop himself from staring. Throughout his long life he'd seen many lovely females, including the four that had mated with his Mag Raith brothers. This lady made all of them pale and vanish from his thoughts.

Was it the pure symmetry of her features that bewitched him? From the elegant wings of her dark red brows to the superb camber of her jaw she seemed unearthly faultless. Glints of gold tipped her auburn lashes. Her full lips, slightly parted, showed a tiny glimpse of teeth like pearls. Surely she had the most beautiful skin he'd ever beheld. To look upon her was to believe in the Gods again, for no hands but those of the almighty ones could have created such a female.

Blindly Kiaran reached for her hand to hold it between his own. "My lady?"

She didn't stir, and when he glanced down he saw small black-inked glyphs covered her right hand from wrist to fingertips. Like him and the rest of the Mag Raith Clan she had been a slave of the Sluath, stolen from her time and taken to their underworld. She must have escaped the demons as they had, with the help of a traitor, and been sent here to be reunited with them.

With me.

Kiaran released her hand to rub his own over his sweating face. All four of the ladies who had found their way back to the Mag Raith had once been lovers with each of his brothers in the underworld. He had been the only one for whom no female had come, which had never greatly concerned him. He'd bedded enough wenches over his long life to satisfy his physical needs, but his heart had never once been stirred by any female. Only now this magnificent lady lay before him, like some boon for a wish he'd never made.

No, she cannae be mine.

Taking hold of the pendant around her neck, Kiaran examined it more closely. It had been fashioned from a carved shell that, like the leather strip, looked very old and worn. He could almost make out a face that had been etched into it, perhaps that of a man. He'd seen similar pendants made by ancient Pritani, usually exchanged and worn by mates. Could she have come from the distant past instead of the future?

Though he had been gentle with the cord, the fragile leather broke. As he pocketed the pendant, he returned his gaze to her face. How long he knelt there studying her Kiaran didn't know. Only when Dive made a sharp sound did he shake off his bewilderment and try to gently wake her again. She remained limp and still, so he would have to carry her back to the stronghold. His arms shook as he reached for her, and lifted her out of the flowers, bringing with her a heady wave of greenery and lilies.

The kestrels took to their wings and hovered, watching him.

The weight of her felt soft rather than heavy against Kiaran's chest, and when he turned to leave the clearing her face touched his neck. He could feel her lips against his skin as if she were kissing him, and it sent a rush of weakness through his belly and legs. At the same time his blood roared in his ears, and his heart pounded like a war drum. He felt more alive than he had since awakening in the ash grove after escaping the Sluath. She might not be his, but she'd made him hers.

Gods help her.

A dream had taken her into a night without end, but now the time to awake had arrived.

Out of that void she climbed, unsteady and hesitant, with nothing more to reassure her than the sense of being held in strong arms. For a time she stopped and stayed between unknowing and knowing, safe in those arms. She had never once experienced that, or such certainty of it, which amazed as much as it comforted her. It also made her question her muddled senses.

Had she truly come out of the darkness? Could she be free of it now?

All that she had left behind her could not wrench her from those arms. She had endured and survived and escaped. She'd be safe now. She had but to open her eyes, and look upon where she had come to, and who had hold of her. Yet doubt still plagued her.

What if 'tis another lie that I told myself?

The chill, damp air moving against her skin stilled and became warmer, and many voices began to speak. First they sounded urgent and jumbled. Several were tough, deep tones blending in surprise. From the movement of those tenors she guessed several men had surrounded her, and she'd been carried into a large chamber where their words echoed faintly. The unfamiliar smells unsettled her, but none of them stank of death. The arms holding her shifted to hold her closer. From the hard chest under her cheek she felt the caress of his melodic voice.

"I found her in the forest."

She opened her eyes, and looked up. Seeing the strong, handsome face and wild mane of red-gold hair surrounding it made her take in a quick breath. The fresh, clean scent of him filled and warmed her, even more so than the blue and white cloth he'd wrapped around her. Everything about him assured her that he was real, and held her close. No place would ever be as safe as she felt in his arms.

Yet all did not seem as it should be. The beautiful light illuminating his features showed them as haggard and drawn, and shadows dulled the dark gems of his eyes.

What makes him so weary?

"My name's Kiaran mag Raith," he said as he bent and gently placed her on a fur by a fire.

When he started to straighten she took hold of his hand, clasping it tightly. She had so much she wished to say that the words crowded and snarled on her tongue until nothing could come out.

"'Twill be well now, lass." Kiaran adjusting the thick cloth covering her bareness. "You've come to Dun Chaill, home of the Mag Raith clan. I shall keep you safe here."

Yes, he would. She could see that in his tired eyes. Now if only she could reassure him. But to give him the same ease was beyond her, especially with her throat so tight she could hardly swallow, much less speak.

Wait. Listen. Breathe.

"Fair morning, my lady," another voice said as a slender shadow stretched over her. The man who joined them had scarlet hair brighter than the flames in the hearth, and vivid blue eyes that shifted over her with intent yet impersonal scrutiny. "I'm Edane mag Raith, our clan's shaman. I shall move aside Kiaran's tartan to check your limbs now. Feel you any pain?"

She shook her head and glanced at the other big men regarding her. Built as large and muscular as Kiaran was, they did not share his particular weariness. Their expressions seemed to her more worried than friendly, but no hatred or anger darkened their eyes. She saw no recognition of her, either.

How was she to feel about that? Dismayed? Hopeful?

Beyond the watching men rose the stone walls of the huge chamber, punctuated with flickering torches. Above her intricately woven boughs had been thatched with neat, tight bundles of grasses still showing green in some places. *Dun Chaill*, Kiaran had called it, which meant "fortress of the lost" in the old tongue.

What shall I lose here?

"I'll fetch our ladies to help," Kiaran said, releasing her hand and moving away before she could stop him.

"I'm Domnall, chieftain of the Mag Raith Clan." The tall man crouched down on her other side, drawing her attention to his stern face. "What name may we call you, my lady?"

The thought of answering him with a lie repelled her. Perhaps admitting that would be enough.

"I cannae say, Chieftain." She saw how her voice startled him as well as the others, but what could she do about that? "'Tis much I dinnae ken."

He exchanged a look with Edane before he

said, "You're Pritani. Remember you the name of your tribe, or their lands?"

Since she had no such memories she shook her head, and looked up as Kiaran returned with four females and another male. Wrapping his tartan around her, she rose and hurried to him. Only when his arms came around her did she let out the breath she'd been holding. As the others moved away, she shivered and pressed closer, hiding her face against him.

"You neednae fear my clan, my lady," Kiaran murmured. "They shall welcome you."

How easily he made such vows when he knew nothing of her. She lifted her head and saw herself reflected in his dark blue eyes, along with a new light. Perhaps he could keep those promises here, in this lost place.

Domnall came to them and introduced each member of the clan. The darkest of the women, Jenna Cameron, he named as his mate. The powerful-looking Mael and stately fair-haired Rosealise also had mated, and served the clan as their seneschal and housekeeper. Edane put his arm around his lady, the small and slender Nellie Quinn, whose friendly smile did not entirely veil the shrewd coolness in her eyes. The darkly handsome Broden and his pale, lean wife Mariena, gave her similar sharp, gauging looks before offering their greetings.

Meeting Kiaran's clan gave her time to calm and stop shaking, but she realized how awkward it would be if she didn't tell them of her dilemma.

"I'd offer my name, Warrior, but I've none," she said to Kiaran, and saw again the flicker of surprise at the sound of her voice. All of them had been expecting someone different, she suspected, someone like the other females, who seemed just as calm and collected as the men. *Ask him for help.* "Mayhap you could give me one?"

"I found you covered in lily flowers." Kiaran took something from her hair—a soft, white bloom—and placed it in her hand. "The old Pritani name for them, 'twould suit you."

She brought the lily to her nose to breathe in its sweet scent, and to hide her pain and relief. At last she had attained that which she had so dearly wanted. "Aye, I should like to be Lilias."

Chapter Two

DEEP BENEATH THE upper levels of Dun Chaill, Cul lurched through the dimly lit tunnels he had hewn himself from the bedrock. Using his tubed listening post to eavesdrop on the clan of intruders had distracted him from the discomfort of his useless leg, but they spoke little in the mornings. Now he dragged the ruined limb behind his misshapen body as he leaned on a thick walking stick, his teeth grinding in unison with every fresh jolt of pain. Any injury he'd suffered in the mortal realm had always been nothing compared to the torments and beatings he had endured as a halfling slave of the Sluath—until now.

His wretched life in the underworld had never made him want to kill himself.

Weeks past he'd not realized how dire his condition would become. After his leg had been crushed in a tower collapse his immortality had healed the shattered bones. Yet they had rejoined wrongly, as if they were a jumble of metal scraps tossed into a forge. Every movement he made caused the jagged mass to tear at the surrounding flesh, which then hardened as it healed, making the next rending that much more painful.

Not even his most powerful potion could dull the hot, throbbing agony now. He might have hacked off the limb to end his misery, but only iron could cut through his flesh. Because he possessed demon as well as mortal blood, the poisoning that the metal inflicted on a Sluath would probably kill him.

I will not go before I have my vengeance.

Cul's vision blurred, and he stopped to brace his shoulder against a stone wall before he swiped at the sweat dripping in his eyes. A glint of light made him squint at one of the viewing mirrors nearby. Positioned with many others to reflect sunlight, they allowed him to watch the great hall during the day. He could see the men gathered near the hearth, and the tartan-draped form of a female. He hobbled a little closer to examine the reflection. It seemed another female slave had escaped the underworld to arrive at Dun Chaill, so now they would be ten. Against an army of demons, they would die just as quickly as nine.

As soon as Kiaran moved away Cul saw the newcomer's dark red hair and stunning features. Shocked to his core, he recoiled from the viewer.

No. It cannot be.

Shadows billowed around him, blotting out the passage as memories of the past thrust him back to his days of serving the Sluath, when they had kept him chained like an animal. To his dismal cell the king's most beautiful slave had come and stood over him, a knowing smirk on her flawless face.

Prince Iolar means to end the king tonight and take the throne. Ye must flee to the mortal realm now or he shall murder ye, too. I shall aid ye.

Why would you save me, little mortal?

She had never answered that question, but she had saved him just the same. If not for her, Cul would never have escaped the underworld, nor found Dun Chaill. To see her here made him tremble, for nothing could have saved her. Iolar surely would have slaughtered her along with the king. No one had despised her more than the prince.

How could she have survived his half-brother's murderous wrath after Cul had escaped?

Cold, damp stone slapped against Cul's face, dragging him from the whirlwind of his thoughts. He pushed himself away from the tunnel wall and watched the mirror image as the clan gathered around his savior. She rose, ran to the falconer, and flung herself against him.

Why was she behaving so fearfully? The slave he dimly remembered had been the favorite of the king, cherished and indulged. Her haughtiness had matched that of the demons. She'd never cowered or quailed like this.

He opened the listening tube next to the mirror station, and heard her accept that flowery name for herself: *Lilias.* Could there be anything less fitting for such a cold, calculating female? Yet she seemed pleased by it, or wanted the clan to believe she was.

Yes, she plays the simple Pritani wench so she can exploit them, just as she did my sire.

Cul had never forgotten his debt to his father's mortal whore. As miserable as his life had been, she had been the instrument of his liberation. Why she'd helped him remained a mystery, for until she came into his cell they had never once spoken.

Nothing he had done since being freed from enslavement could have been possible without her intervention. He could never harm her.

The voices of the clan went silent, and when he checked the mirror again he saw the great hall standing empty. Doubtless the clan now rallied around Lilias, for they believed her to be like them. They had no idea what she truly was, or just how dangerous she could be.

"If only Iolar had seen you fall from the sky bridge," Cul muttered, and then a rough laugh burst from his tight throat as he imagined his half-brother's reaction. The prince believed her long dead, and if he ever saw her again nothing would stop him from coming for her.

Fate had delivered to Cul the final tool with which he would take his vengeance. No enticement could be as perfect as Lilias to lure Iolar and his demons into Dun Chaill.

Chapter Three

DOMNALL WATCHED LILIAS'S flawless face as Jenna persuaded her to go with her and find some proper garments to wear. Although she resembled a goddess made flesh, her shy silence reassured him. Most females from his tribe had been as modest and quiet before strangers. Kiaran seemed entirely focused on her, even enchanted, a development the chieftain welcomed as much as the lady's presence. The clan had all been worried about their falconer, who had grown distant and silent over the summer. That Lilias seemed to be inclined toward him boded well for them both.

Since coming to Dun Chaill, however, the

chieftain had learned the peril of assuming that all was what it appeared, or promised to be.

"Nellie and I will go and prepare a chamber for our new guest," Rosealise said. "She may wish to wash and dress in privacy."

"We'll be in the forge working on the fortifications," Domnall told her, and glanced at the Frenchwoman, who nodded in silent understanding.

"The lady seems a rare beauty," Mael said once they entered the spell-protected forge, the only place inside the stronghold where they could speak freely. "Such a fetching female must have been greatly prized by her kin."

"Aye, so 'tis odd that none of us ever heard of such a lass." Usually the wariest of outsiders, Broden sounded more puzzled than scathing. "Much was said of my looks among the Mag Raith and their neighboring tribes, and she outshines me like the sun. More, why doesnae she recall her name? Our other ladies did, even when naught else remained in their memories."

"She may be too fearful or shocked by her ordeal," Edane said. "She's a timid thing. To be stolen from her time by demons, and enslaved in the underworld—doubtless 'twas much for a Pritani female to endure."

The trapper grunted. "Or she's chosen no' to reveal what she remembers, as did my wife."

Mariena placed her slim hand on Broden's arm. "Perhaps like me she has good reason to say nothing, *mon couer*."

"Lilias only just arrived, and doesnae ken any of us," Mael suggested. "We cannae force the lass to view us as her kinsmen. We must earn her trust."

"If she's our kin at all," Broden said, and then he sighed. "I'm too suspicious, I reckon. She seems a sweet and gentle lass, but something about her doesnae feel like the females of the tribe."

The shaman's brows drew together. "In truth I saw no skinwork on her other than the Sluath glyphs covering her right hand. All grown Pritani lasses bore spirit markings."

"Some western tribes didnae permit their females to offer themselves to the spirits," Domnall reminded him. "She may hail from the midlands. Or mayhap the demons took her before she came of age to choose." He regarded Kiaran, whose silence troubled him. "You've no memory of the lass?"

"None." As always the falconer sounded indifferent, but something in the way he held himself hinted of tightly-leashed emotion.

Or pain. Whatever burden plagued the falconer had grown heavy in these last weeks, that much the chieftain sensed. Yet as he had since coming to the Mag Raith tribe as a lad, Kiaran would likely remain aloof, and keep his concerns to himself.

Domnall wished he had more time to delve into the falconer's troubles, and discuss with his clan what to do with Lilias, but they had far more serious worries.

"Now that Galan has discovered Dun Chaill, we must prepare for him to return with the Sluath. They shall likely wait for a storm so they may fly to attack us, but we cannae take thus for granted." He regarded Broden and Mariena. "I've made you our war masters for good reason. You've the canniest minds among the clan. Aside from blocking the entries to the castle, how may we better our chances against the demons?"

"Even with your ability to fly and all of our powers, there are not enough of us to take on the demons," the Frenchwoman said. "We must use the castle."

Broden produced a scroll, which he rolled out on Kiaran's work table.

"My lady copied this from the map of the stronghold," the trapper said as he swept his hand over the detailed sketch. "Here you see the towers, chambers and store rooms. We rig doors that we can draw open with hidden ropes at these outer entries." He pointed to narrow access points on three sides of the castle. "We choose when the Sluath enter Dun Chaill."

Mael's brows rose. "You'd *permit* the demons come inside?"

"Only where we wish them to, *mon ami*," Mariena said. "We change the passages, building false walls and new archways. They will channel the Sluath to the vine room, the mill house, and the fire tunnel. Once inside each chamber, the demons' presence shall activate the spells, sealing them inside. Our shaman must then aid us so that the Sluath are properly welcomed."

Edane nodded. "The vine room remains wholly intact, and 'twould be naught to reset the trigger spells in the fire tunnel. Yet you destroyed the mill stones, Broden."

"After I cleared out the stone, Mariena and I found that the rollers and shafts still work," the trapper said. "I shall fit the moving mounts with new panels spiked with iron stakes."

Mael grimaced before he leaned over the table and tapped a spot outside the kitchen walls. "Outside we might place straw sentinels dressed as the clan inside the hedgerows. 'Twould lure the Sluath into the killing maze."

"No' all the demons shall be caught in the traps or tricked by your hay men," Kiaran said suddenly. "What then?"

"'Tis why we shall need you and your wee screechers," Broden said. "You'll patrol from above, and send your kestrels after the Sluath that escape. The clan shall emerge from hiding in the trees to pursue and end them."

"The women and I will take position in the new tower," Mariena said, "inside shielded blinds at the window slits here." She indicated the place on the scroll. "We'll have crossbows with iron-tipped arrows to bring down the strays."

Domnall took another moment to study the details of the sketch. "'Tis a shrewd plan, but 'twill require much work by the clan quickly done. Since 'tis their scheme, Broden and Mariena shall take charge and direct us." He looked up at Edane. "While the clan works, you and your lady should continue your search of the stronghold for Culvar's hiding place."

"Mariena," Kiaran said, "when the demons come you'll keep Lilias protected?"

"But of course, *mon ami*," she said nodding. "Though I would prefer to join you in battle, I must agree with my husband. We will be most lethal from the tower. Lilias will be safe with us."

The falconer's scowl eased. "She's fearful, but I reckon she'll give you no trouble. She's a sweet, gentle lass."

"I'm inclined to agree, but she doesnae ken the stronghold," Domnall told him. "Until the Sluath attack, she's yours to watch."

Kiaran's expression emptied as he looked away. "She'd fare better among the other ladies. I've naught for her."

"Brother," Broden muttered softly, as if warning him.

"You've naught for anyone of late." Domnall stepped closer, forcing him to meet his gaze. "From pity I've ignored your coldness, and the distance you've put between us, but no longer. The Sluath come, and we face a battle that shall likely decide our fate. We live or die as one clan. If you're done with the Mag Raith, take your kestrels and be gone with you. If you remain our brother in truth, then do your part. What choose you, Kiaran?"

"I'm Mag Raith," the falconer said, sounding tired now. "I'll do as you command, Chieftain."

Chapter Four

THE SOUND OF demons bickering woke Iolar from his thin, unsatisfying rest. The airless, dank cave in the ridges to which he'd retreated now echoed with their snide voices, clawing at the inside of his skull like so many burrowing carrion beetles.

"When we return to the underworld, we should write an account of our great suffering." As dulcet and innocent as a child's, the voice belonged to Meirneal, the smallest of the Sluath. "I think it should begin with how Prince Iolar commanded his legions to journey to the mortal realm to cull the souls of spineless humans. And so, we did, again and again, with great success, until this time."

"It's not our fault," Clamhan muttered, his voice muffled by the partial human skull he always wore as a mask to terrify humans. "One of our own went mad, betrayed us and trapped us here by sealing off every gate to the underworld."

Iolar came fully out of his resting state, and folded his white and gold wings before dropping down to the stone floor. His immortal body, perfect and inviolate, trembled now with weakness. Here and there unfamiliar aches throbbed in his joints. When he held his hands out into a shaft of light he saw how dull his flesh had grown. Tiny cracks were forming along the sides of his talons.

Retreating into silence and darkness should have fully restored the Sluath prince, as it always had before. The fact that it hadn't done so meant the degeneration would continue and grow worse.

"You should add that the Sluath faced slow starvation and madness, until His Majesty used his unparalleled power to save us all," the shape-shifting Seabhag said, his tone changing from feminine to masculine as doubtless his form did the same.

"And when did our prince do that?" Meirneal cooed with acid sweetness. "In your dreams?"

Rarely had Iolar retreated from the village

they had occupied since becoming trapped in the mortal realm. For his demons to dare intrude on his solitude here promised nothing pleasurable for him.

"What matters is that if we stay here we will wither and die, and that will be our end," Clamhan said over the sounds of the other demons bickering. "Or that traitorous tree-licker has found the means with which to slaughter us all."

"If you keep whining, *I* will kill you all," Danar said. He had the deepest voice among them. "Shut your mouths." The others obeyed. "We haven't kept accounts of our culls since we burned the old king's library. We will not be trapped here forever. Stop squabbling over nonsense."

"Maybe if we still had the old scrolls," Seabhag countered, "we'd know how to build a new gate to the underworld."

Dead leaves crunched beneath Iolar's boots as he emerged from the cave into the glare of morning. His appearance silenced his four most trusted *deamhanan*, and for a moment they formed a still life of petulant discontent. That made him imagine taking up Danar's suggestion and slaughtering them all.

Each of these Sluath had failed him miserably, and yet they still came to regale him with new tales of their latest ineptitude. Was this why he had orchestrated his father's murder and seized the throne? To rule over bungling fools who could not carry out the simplest task he asked of them? He should tear them to pieces.

What stayed his hand was knowing these to be the cleverest of his demons. Killing them might very well extend his exile in this dreary world forever.

Iolar regarded Danar, the largest and most lethal of the Sluath. A study in earthen colors and immense strength, the big *deamhan* served at his right hand. "What now?"

Hundreds of blades strapped to the demon's harnessed wings glittered in the sunlight as he bowed.

"The druid has returned, my prince. He awaits you in the village." Danar hesitated before he added, "He claims the Mag Raith butchered all of the enslaved humans he took with him."

Galan Aedth had amused and annoyed Iolar since the moment the Sluath had first encountered the druid hunting the Pritani rebels. How quickly he had offered to serve as their ally in return for his dead wife's resurrection. How easily he had been duped into believing Iolar would do so for him. The dark-hearted druid's greed for power ran as deep as his stupidity, or so the prince had assumed. Still, he would miss sporting with Galan, but the time to end this game had arrived.

Meirneal crept a little closer, his fair curls framing a cunningly sweet face. "Please let me have Aedth, Magnificence. If you take back the Sluath power you bestowed on him, he'll still be mortal enough to torment. I'm the most skilled at that."

Iolar gazed down at the small demon, whose hunger for human flesh far exceeded his childlike size. Dark stains mottled Meirneal's limp, soiled, pastel garments, and he stank of rot. "Have you been eating the dead again?"

"I can't help it, my prince." The cherubic smile slipped. "We can't feed on souls here, and there aren't any breathing humans left now."

All of the other demons appeared just as disheveled and sickly. Even Danar, the strongest *deamhan* among the horde, had developed a new pallid caste to his dark skin. They had been too long exiled. If they did not soon return to the underworld, all the Sluath would begin to alter in even more unpleasant ways. Since the signs on Iolar's own body indicated that he would share the same fate, he felt no pity for his ailing demons.

"You will have to feed on what you can in this cesspool. Their fear," he told Meirneal, "not their flesh." He took in the rest with a sweeping gaze. "Send hunters to obtain some mortals from the midlands tonight. Make sure they find a pretty wench for me. No one touches the druid unless I give the order."

Iolar stalked back to the village, where he saw a shimmer of magic just beyond the outer most cottages. It grew brighter the closer he came, until it curved in on itself to form a spherical ward around the tall, dark figure of Galan Aedth. It radiated the power the prince had given to the druid to restore his ability to cast spells, which ironically he now employed to protect himself against the Sluath.

Stopping a few inches from the ward, Iolar peered inside at his troublesome protégé. The druid appeared calm and focused. His thin lips formed an insincere smile as he looked over the prince and the demons following him. Galan had fed his vanity by dressing in his finest robes and arranging his hair like a gleaming black mane around his arrogant features.

"The prodigal traitor returns." Iolar made a point to look around the druid as if expecting more. "Empty-handed yet again."

"Fair morning." Galan inclined his head as if they were equals. "I bring news you've long awaited. I've found where the Mag Raith hide."

The druid's smug discourtesy didn't unsettle Iolar as much as the confidence that glittered in his dark eyes. As he heard Danar drawing blades he made a subtle motion with his claws, signaling the big demon to hold back.

"Congratulations, Aedth." He smiled back. "No doubt you expect something in return for this information."

"I want the skinwork you gave to the Pritani and their sluts," Galan said evenly, and before Iolar replied held up a warning hand. "Dinnae attempt to again mislead me. I ken 'tis what resurrects them. I saw your ink revive the pale wench after she'd nearly been torn apart. Once I've the tattoo, I shall tell you where to find the Mag Raith. They're protected by magic even more powerful than yours. End me, and you'll never find them."

"Your bargaining skills are as sharp as ever, Aedth. Very well. You'll have what you want." Iolar turned his back on the druid and met the startled gazes of his demons, shaking his head slightly before regarding Danar. "Come and prepare the ink with me."

Once inside the hovel the prince had been forced to occupy during their exile, Danar's expression went from neutral to perplexed. "You know what will happen if we mark Galan now, my prince."

"Oh, yes. I've so looked forward to it." Iolar tossed some wood into the fire dying in the hearth. "After he reveals where we may find the Mag Raith, cut his throat and throw him in the charnel pit."

Chapter Five

KIARAN LEFT THE forge to return to the great hall, where Rosealise had set out two steaming mugs and a platter of oatcakes and berries. Since he'd missed the clan's morning meal, he assumed it was meant for him and Lilias. Once the changes had come over him he'd had no desire for food. Still he'd forced himself to eat, hoping it would stave off what had been happening to him. Now the scent of honey-sweetened brew and fruit made his stomach clench, but not with revulsion.

For the first time in weeks he felt hungry.

"Oh, good, you're here." Jenna came into the hall with Nellie, and the two women parted as

Kiaran turned to face them. "You see, Lilias? I told you that he wouldn't go far."

The Pritani woman stepped forward, her lovely face flushed and her hands tucked under her arms. The ladies had dressed her in a simple gown of light cream wool, and draped her shoulders with his blue and white tartan. The garments made her skin look rosy-golden. A pair of Jenna's fur-lined boots now graced her long, narrow feet, and one of Mariena's reed whistles hung from her neck like a pendant. She still smelled faintly of the lilies from the meadow.

His brother's mates had also gathered Lilias's gleaming dark red hair into a thick braid that now hung down to her waist. With the care the ladies had taken with her she looked even more like a goddess, but it was seeing her wrapped in his plaid that made his hands itch to touch her again.

By the Gods.

Kiaran's hunger sharpened, but he no longer wanted food.

What does she to me?

"'Twas kind of your ladies to offer me their garments, Warrior." Lilias glanced down at herself before she met his gaze. "I shall make my own as soon as I may."

"Don't worry about that, Sister," Nellie said, her sharp eyes shifting to Kiaran's face. "We've got plenty of duds to share. Jenny, maybe you and I should go hunt down your man and see what's what."

Before Kiaran could protest, the two ladies turned and exited, leaving him alone with Lilias.

"If you're needed by the clan, Warrior, I shall wait here," she assured him, her tone soft. She touched the whistle she wore. "Lady Jenna showed me how to use this to summon aid if I'm in need."

Need, aye. I'll give you what you need.

Kiaran's lustful reaction to her innocent remark made him wish he could leave her there, but he'd given his word to the chieftain. Whatever the lass made him feel mattered little. She need never know of his yearning.

"No, my lady. I'm to…show you the stronghold and the surroundings." Fack, but he would not act the beardless lad around her. He turned and went to the trestle table. "You'll want first to break your fast."

She came and sat down beside him on the bench, and looked at the meal as if unsure of what to do with it.

"Rosealise takes great pains with her brews. 'Twas part of a ritual with much weight in her time." Kiaran filled mugs for them both, and selected the choicest of the fruit and cakes, placing them in a trencher before her.

Some of the tension left her shoulders, but she still didn't touch the food.

Kiaran had been among women from future times for so long he'd forgotten how those from the tribes behaved. Among the ancient Pritani, males always ate before females, who served them. He'd probably confused her by doing that.

"You neednae wait for me," he assured her. "'Tisnae the clan's custom. We view our ladies as our equals. Eat as you wish."

Delicately Lilias picked up a strawberry, bringing it to her nose before she nibbled at the end. The juice stained her lips as she stiffened, her eyes widening. She then popped the whole berry into her mouth and reached for another.

Seeing her pleasure made Kiaran consider not eating just so he could enjoy watching her. She ate as if she had never before tasted such simple delights. It added to his secret torment, but it felt good to suffer something other than self-disgust. Perhaps she had forgotten the taste of fruit along with everything else in her past. As he didn't wish to make her uncomfortable with his staring, he took an oatcake for himself. That lead to another, and soon he was piling berries atop more as he filled his own empty belly.

At last they emptied the platter and the brew pitcher, which made Kiaran sigh. "'Twas good. I've no' had much appetite of late."

Lilias set down her mug, saying nothing but regarding him with visible curiosity.

A Pritani female would never question a male, he recalled from the time of his mortal life, or speak out of turn. Among the Mag Raith tribe, women waited to hear whatever their fathers, brothers or mates cared to tell them. He wasn't her man, although Domnall's order made Kiaran responsible for her.

For all the many tasks he'd performed for the Mag Raith he'd never looked after a female, and had little idea of how to do so. He wanted to put her at ease, yet had no inkling of what would reassure her. He'd never paid any attention to what the other hunters' wives said over their meals unless they spoke directly to him. At least in that he and Lilias were much alike.

The straps beneath his tunic tightened along with his shoulders.

No matter. She'll despise me soon enough.

"We shouldnae leave more work for our housekeeper," Kiaran said, rising from the bench. "Come with me, my lady."

Wordlessly she helped him carry the dishes into the kitchens, and helped him with the washing. As they worked side by side he considered just what he had agreed to. Keeping his word to Domnall meant Kiaran now would spend most of his time in the stronghold as Lilias adjusted to living at Dun Chaill. He thought of Galan and the demons.

However long that shall be.

How like his wretched luck for Lilias to arrive at the castle at this moment in time.

After finishing in the kitchens Kiaran showed Lilias around the castle, and pointed out the chambers and areas with traps to avoid before accompanying her outside. Sending a command to his kestrels to keep their distance, he guided her through the gardens and warned her about the hedge maze. While she looked at everything with wide eyes, she listened closely and easily kept pace with him. Her quiet presence proved a welcome relief from the chattering he usually tolerated from the other hunters when he patrolled with them.

It was only after they'd walked the length of a patrol of the outer walls that he realized just how quiet Lilias had been. She hadn't said one word to him since offering to wait alone in the hall.

"You may say or ask anything of me, my lady, whenever you wish," Kiaran said, stopping by the pasture fence so she could look out at their bountiful herds. When she didn't reply he added, "You must be curious about the clan and the castle, or what brought us to Dun Chaill. Did Lady Jenna tell you of the demons?"

Lilias gazed at the fat sheep and cattle for a long moment before she regarded him. "Aye, the chieftain's wife told me of the Sluath. They're more powerful than the old Pritani legends. They took your clan out of time to serve as their slaves, and forced you to suffer grievous torments."

He felt startled by this revelation, and yet glad to know Jenna had revealed the truth to the lass. In the past too much grief had been caused among the clan by withholding the truth of their circumstances. "What more said she?"

"Being taken changed your clan. You do not

grow sick or old, and cannae easily die." Her golden-brown eyes shifted over his face. "You've lost your memories, but gained great talents. All of your clan and their ladies mated in the underworld, forgot their love after they fled, and yet found each other again here."

"Lady Jenna told you all, then," he said, even as he wondered if Domnall's mate had also mentioned how he had been changed.

"She said your castle, 'tis protected by magic, but the mad druid who betrayed you discovered you here. Soon he and the demons shall come, and 'twill be a terrible battle. The clan prepares now to fight them." Her lips thinned, and she took in a shaky breath. "'Tis so much I hardly ken what to reckon."

Without thinking Kiaran reached out to touch her shoulder. Recalling at the last moment how cold his flesh had grown, he stopped himself. "You shouldnae fear. I shall…the clan shall protect you."

"Should the Sluath prevail, at least I may die as you live here," Lilias said, her voice dropping to a low murmur as she looked down at her marked hand. "Free of them."

Dread swamped him as he saw the tightness

of her jaw, and heard the huskiness in her tone. If she began weeping it would be worse than what he'd endured when he'd used his heated sword on his back. Lilias also needed to know she had strong allies among the Mag Raith.

"We've fought long and hard for our freedom, my lady," Kiaran told her. "We shall permit naught to take that from us, or you."

Her expression eased. "I feel the same. Whatever I may do to help, you've but to ask."

"Do you ride?" When she held up her palms in a helpless gesture he moved away from the fence. "Come. We shall learn if you did."

In the stables he selected and bridled the calmest of the clan's mares. He placed a sturdy saddle on her while Lilias stood to one side and observed him.

"In your time you likely rode bareback, if at all," he told her as he secured the girth strap. "'Twill seem odd at first, but relax and dinnae resist the motion as the mare moves."

"'Tisnae familiar to me," she said, looking unsure.

He beckoned her closer, and as soon as she came within the horse's reach the mare tried to nuzzle her neck as if they were old friends.

"Already she favors you," Kiaran told her when he saw her stiffen in reaction to the horse's show of affection. "Stroke her in return, just so."

Gingerly she ran her hand along the neck as he demonstrated. The mare rubbed her head against Lilias's cheek and whickered with contentment.

"Oh," Lilias whispered. "You're a kind one." Her eyes closed for a moment as she returned the caress.

"You've the touch with animals." He'd never expected to feel envious of a horse, but seeing her delight in the animal's response made his resentment fade. "Now you must mount her."

Moving around the mare, Lilias studied the saddle for a moment, and then looked into the animal's placid dark eyes. A moment later she stepped up onto the stump the other ladies used for their horses. Taking hold of the front horn, she nimbly seated herself and picked up the reins.

All of the other women had needed some time to learn how to ride with the clan's leather-clad wooden tack, which Jenna called "primitive" and Rosealise "barbaric." Nellie, who had spent her childhood on a farm, preferred not to use a saddle at all. Yet here Lilias sat, as much at ease as if born on horseback.

Quickly Kiaran saddled his own gelding, and then walked the horse ahead of Lilias and the mare, who followed him out at a sedate pace. He saw that the lass knew enough to rein in the horse once they had cleared the stable doors. Outside he mounted, and pointed to the widest trail around the castle.

"Keep to my side, and we'll ride patrol together to the river and back," he told her.

"Aye." She came alongside him, and peered at the trail. "How shall I ken the river?"

"'Tis long and wet," he joked, and then saw her worried expression. *She doesnae recall what means the word.* "'Tis a wide, deep stream that runs through the land to the east of Dun Chaill. We'll stop there to water the mounts."

Lilias nodded quickly. "Forgive me, 'tis much I dinnae ken of this place."

Chapter Six

SEARCHING THE STRONGHOLD for Culvar's hiding place while pretending to work didn't bother Nellie Quinn. Being an undercover Prohibition agent in her own time had required her to pretend to be a carefree flapper for years. That had made it possible to secretly hunt the illegal speakeasies for her brother's killers.

Her husband Edane, however, didn't have a devious bone in his body. More than once that morning he forgot to keep up their ruse.

"You're the keenest, Danny," Nellie told him after she pushed him inside the forge to have a talk. "But you've got to stop poking and prodding every wall we pass. We know Culvar can spy on us, and he'll get wise to our operation."

"I'm a hunter, my *peyrl*. No' a copper." The shaman tugged her into his arms, kissing her brow before searching her eyes. "'Tis more on your mind than my clumsiness."

Even when she put on her gladdest mug, her man always sensed when she was out of sorts, another reason she loved him. He got her like nobody ever had or would—and that gave her an idea.

"I need to get the slant on Lilias." She nudged him. "You still got that pendant the Pritani gal was wearing?"

Edane frowned. Kiaran had turned it over to him at the chieftain's request. Though Edane had found no trace of spellwork on it, he'd yet to give it back.

"'Twill show you naught good."

Nellie didn't like using her ability to see the past by touching objects. Yet she was the Mag Raith's copper, and something about Lilias made her feel as if she should be antsy—not that she was. She liked the pretty Pritani woman, who seemed as sweet and gentle as a lamb. Lilias had also taken an instant shine to Kiaran, which pleased Nellie. Without a mate of his own the falconer had been a sad sap, close to taking a bounce from the clan.

Besides that, Kiaran needed to suffer a little, Nellie thought darkly. He'd certainly put her and Edane through the wringer.

"You'll be right here if I go all crazy like the first time I walked into the castle." She held out her hand. "Just grab me if I do so I don't conk myself out again."

Very reluctantly Edane took out the carved shell pendant, but held it up out of her reach. "You'll tell me all, Wife."

She blew him a saucy kiss. "Sure thing, Husband."

The moment he placed the old necklace on her palm, Nellie felt the cold rush of her ability spread through her. The forge and Edane faded from her vision, replaced by a glaring blue-white light that made her stomach sink.

She stood in an underworld chamber filled with dazzling treasures. All around her piles of jewels and coins and precious objects had been heaped in huge, glittering mounds around heavy chests and graceful urns. She turned to see a row of silver cages filled with exotic birds, their bright plumage still visible beneath the ice that held them captive. A rack of gorgeous gowns embroidered with silks and pearls stood to one side, opposite another laden with dozens of sleek furs.

Beyond the priceless hoard she saw rows of slaves, each frozen in place. Dozens of beautiful females and handsome males, all dressed in finery from different times, had been stashed like presents. All of them stared back at her with empty eyes.

I've been here before. Dimly she recalled being shoved into this room by Danar just after she'd come to the underworld. *This is the king's treasure room.*

Edane had worked with her on keeping her emotions in check when she used her ability, but Nellie felt herself shaking as she moved forward. She saw herself stretched out on a velvet fainting divan, idly waving a feather fan back and forth in front of her face. That other Nellie still wore the blood-stained dress she'd had on when she'd gotten shot in the speakeasy where Danar had taken her.

"You're going to have to talk to me some time," she heard herself say in a raspy voice, as if she'd been talking too much. "We can't just sit here staring at each other for the rest of however long they keep us locked up."

Across from her sat Lilias, magnificent in a black sheath dress covered with gold-colored jewels. Her hair had been artfully arranged around a tiara with a yellow diamond the size of a hen's egg, and smaller matching gems glittered in her ears. The demons had manacled her arms and legs to the walls with heavy chains.

"Why would ye care to speak to me, Demon?" Lilias asked.

"I told you, Sister, I'm not one of them," Nellie said, and yawned. "And I don't care about you. I'm just bored. Why did they stick you in this hoosgow? Ain't you playing nice with the palookas?"

"I ever do what they wish." Lilias glanced around them. "Here, 'tis where I live now."

Nellie saw pity fill her own eyes. "What's your name, Sister?"

Darkness engulfed the treasure room, and when the light returned Nellie saw Lilias in a scarlet hooded cloak standing over a crumpled heap in a filthy slave's tunic. Although it was obviously herself there on the floor, she had no memory of the encounter.

"You mustnae refuse Danar's orders, Helen," Lilias was saying as she helped her up. "He shall whip you next time, or force you to hurt one of the taken."

Shocked to hear the Pritani slave use her real name, Nellie almost missed the fact that Lilias said *you* instead of *ye*. How much time had passed?

"They're doing that to the ones who sound like you. Big guys. Well, all but one. He's probably not going to make it, poor sap." As her hands touched the cloak, Slave Nellie went still and stared at the Pritani woman. "Holy moly. You went alone? Have you lost your marbles?"

"I promised I'd deliver a message," the Pritani woman told her, sounding slightly terrified all the same. "Helen, 'tis something I must tell you."

Shadows again filled the room, thinning only once more to show Lilias holding Nellie as she wept against her shoulder. Both of them again wore different garments. The room filled with sparkling white light, and Prince Iolar entered.

"This is why you do not come when I call for

you?" He picked up Nellie and tossed her away as he loomed over the Pritani woman. "Danar, come and get your touch-reader. She's meddling with my treasure."

"Don't you touch her," Nellie shrieked, only to be clouted again.

Utter blackness slammed down, and a heartbeat later Nellie found herself back in the forge with Edane, who now held the pendant in his fist. Shivs of pain went off in her head as they always did whenever she tried to remember something.

"You've looked enough," he told her as he wrapped his tartan and then his arms around her, and only then did she feel how cold she'd become, and the uncontrollable way she was shaking. "'Twas too much."

"No, I'm aces." Nellie huddled against him. "Just hold me. You can pet me, too, if you want."

"I should thrash you." Edane kissed her temple, and rubbed the plaid over her shivering limbs. "You vowed to me you'd stop being reckless now that we've mated."

Nellie tipped her head back to look into the vivid blue heaven of his eyes. "And you believed me, you sap."

It took her a few minutes to get warm and

calm again, and then she told him what she had seen.

"They locked up Lilias with me in the underworld." She pressed her numb fingers against her aching brow. "She's the prince's treasure. You know, the one he accused me of stealing."

"She's a beauty to be sure, but why would he think her a treasure?"

"I don't know." Nellie grimaced. "I didn't see all of what she went through there. She tried to tell me something, but then things went black. After that, time seemed to jump ahead."

"Mariena said that the traitorous demon who sent us here took our memories from us," Edane reminded her. "Lilias likely endured the same."

"That's not it." Nellie realized something else. "I remember more about the underworld than anyone else in the clan. I spent nearly a century as a Sluath slave, and I remember you and me, and the others, and escaping—but not Lilias. Before I touched that pendant I didn't have a single memory of her. Yet she called me Helen, so we must have been close friends. I really liked her. I tried to protect her from that louse Iolar."

He touched her cold cheek. "I dinnae ken why that troubles you."

"I still can't tell you *why* I liked her. I also got the feeling that we spent a lot of time in that treasure room," Nellie told him. "Like maybe decades. So why would the traitor make me forget all of that?"

Chapter Seven

AT THE RIVER Kiaran dismounted, watching Lilias as she did the same. She nearly lost her footing as she stared at the rushing water, her perfect lips rounding with surprise. Her hand trembled as she took hold of the mare's bridle and led her to a drop-off where she could drink.

There she crouched down beside her mount and regarded the bubbling currents with absorbed fascination.

He guided his gelding beside the mare before he came to stand over the Pritani woman. "'Tis a pretty spot."

"Aye." Reluctantly she stood and took in the glen and ridges beyond the river's banks. "Had I the skill, I'd build a *broch* just here, so that I might wake each morn to such peace and beauty."

"You'd regret thus when the snows come, and the river turns to ice." When she shook her head Kiaran frowned. "You dinnae favor living in the stronghold with the clan?"

"Oh, no." She gave him a sideways glance. "I owe them much for their kindness and care. I must do what I may to show gratitude."

How like a woman of the tribe to be more concerned with the desires of others, but her careful reply didn't fool him.

"'Tis the ladies, I reckon," he said. "In their times they didnae dwell in tribes. They tell us that females of the future live and work on their own, as bold and free as males. Mariena served her people as a warrior."

Lilias looked startled. "Truly?"

"Aye. The chieftain made her war master along with Broden." He picked up a stone and tossed it into the currents. "Our other ladies possess many talents as well. Yet as much as I admire them, they can be…quite clamorous."

"'They scarce take breath when they speak with me." Her face reddened. "By the time I answer one question, they've asked three more."

"Truth." He'd never expected that she would feel as he did about all the chatter. "Mayhap I shall build a *broch* beside yours, that I too might delight in the quiet."

A flicker of hope passed over her enchanting features before she turned and caught the mare's reins as the mount finished drinking. She then used a boulder on the bank to climb up into the saddle before shyly meeting his gaze.

Mounting his gelding, Kiaran nodded toward the forest to the south of the stronghold. "If you're no' weary, next I'll show you the boundaries of the spell barrier, so you ken where you mustnae go."

They spent the remainder of the morning and most of the afternoon riding a complete circuit of the wall of magic that shielded Dun Chaill against the demons. Although Kiaran said little, and Lilias even less, the silence they shared never felt oppressive. Indeed, he'd never felt such contentment while in a female's company. By the time they rode back to the stables, he almost dreaded the thought of joining the clan for the evening meal.

"My thanks for the ride, Warrior," Lilias said as she unsaddled the mare. "'Twas pleasing, but

I'll see to the horses. I shouldnae keep you from your duties any longer."

"You're my duty, my lady," Kiaran said flatly. When she looked horrified he quickly added, "The chieftain doesnae wish you to come to harm, so I'm to accompany you." He took the saddle from her and set it on the drying rack.

"Oh." Her shoulders slumped. "I hadnae reckoned."

"If you wish another, I shall ask," he told her, at the same time she said, "I'd no' be a burden to you."

They both fell silent. A hen wandered through the doors, clucking as it pecked at the straw strewn on the floor for stray grain. When it reached Kiaran's boot toe it straightened, looked up at him, squawked loudly and flew out of the stables.

"There, that 'tis my one true burden," he said, as if greatly aggrieved. "I terrify chickens."

"'Tis a weighty hindrance," Lilias said, her tone solemn. "I cannae fathom how you bear such a fault."

"I dinnae gather eggs," he admitted. "Nor muck out the hen house. Neither would survive my attempts, you see." He faced her, and saw how she was pressing her lips together. "'Tisnae amusing. No matter how deeply I long for such joys, they're forever denied me."

A small chuckle escaped her before she cleared her throat. "Never again shall I feel a burden to you, Warrior."

"Kiaran." He wanted to hear her say his name. "You neednae be so formal with me."

"As you say…Kiaran." His name left her lips with a sigh of pleasure. "My thanks."

He looked at her for a long moment, and then by unspoken agreement they went to finish caring for their mounts.

Chapter Eight

AFTER THE EVENING meal Jenna and Rosealise took Lilias with them to the clan's bathing chamber, leaving Kiaran some time to retreat to his tower and attend to himself and his kestrels. After being commanded to stay away from him and Lilias for the day, Dive and the other raptors swooped down as soon as they spied him, all of them alighting to perch on his shoulders, head and arms.

"'Tis good to ken you missed me," Kiaran told the little female, who responded with a low chittering greeting. Although he knew her primitive thoughts and emotions through his power, as alpha Dive showed dominance to the others through the exchange of sounds. "I reckoned my absence might gladden you."

The kestrel uttered a shrill sound, nipping his wrist with her sharp beak before she met his gaze and extended her wings in a regal show before bowing her head in submission. She had no words in her mind, but showed him a memory of himself as a lad, reaching to free her from brambles. That simple act of kindness had bonded them forever.

Like her life, her loyalty to him would never end.

Sensing their hunger, Kiaran directed half the flight to go hunting, and the rest to patrol the skies above Dun Chaill. He then went into the ruined tower, where he filled his wash basin and took out clean garments. Glancing toward the curtain separating his room from the rest of the tower, he pulled off his tunic. His back felt as if he'd been subjected to a slow thrashing with bramble canes, but that had been his doing. Wincing, he began releasing the straps of the tight harness he now had to wear to keep the shield on his back in place.

The clan believed he'd stopped using their bathing chamber because he preferred his solitude, when in truth he sought to conceal what none of them yet knew.

As Kiaran hunched over to remove the wide, flat shield that covered most of his spine, the aching flesh beneath it sprang free and stretched out on either side of him. Turning his head, he still could not see the tips, but each day they grew longer. He felt the skin itching where tiny quills had recently pushed out. With great difficulty he'd manage to tug out one of the small feathers, which proved to be red-gold, the same color as his hair.

Soon his new wings would grow too large to cram under the shield.

Reaching for the catch of his sword belt made Kiaran stop and rest his hand on the hilt of his blade. He'd cut off the first beginnings of wings to grow on his back, much to Edane's disgust. The second growth had begun some days after his wounds had healed, making him realize the futility of trying to hack away the demon flesh. He could spend the rest of eternity carving up his body, he suspected, but it would not change what was happening to him. He simply repeated the vow he had taken when he'd realized what he was to become.

I shall end myself before I change fully into a demon.

The prospect of taking his own life had never troubled him. Kiaran had come to accept his dilemma as the price of his many betrayals. Yet since Lilias had come to Dun Chaill he found himself despising the terrible choices he had made since the night he'd watched his tribe's village burn.

I'll never merit love.

He washed quickly, donning the back shield again and grimacing as he fought to strap down the wings so they would not bulge out under his tunic. Each time it grew more painful to bind them, but he also considered that suffering his due. Had he any true valor, he'd fall on his sword this moment and let the iron blade cleave his worthless heart in two. Yet that same choice had been his as a lad, and like a craven coward he'd run from it.

Mayhap if I'd gone back with my sire, I'd never have damned my brothers. I'd only have blackened my own soul.

"Kiaran?"

His head jerked up at the sound of Broden's call, and he fumbled with the straps before yanking on a too-large tunic. "Aye, here." That he still felt fear gave him a little hope that he'd slowed the changes, for he knew the demons felt nothing but hatred and greed. "Give me a moment, Brother."

"I've seen you unclad," the trapper said on the other side of the curtain. "'Tis no' that I'm desirous to gaze again upon your bare arse, you ken, but the chieftain bid me lay eyes on you." After a short pause he asked, "You've no' sprouted claws nor horns this day?"

With a surge of impatience Kiaran tugged aside the curtain. "As you see." He made a show of pulling up and lacing his trews. "I've washed the stink of horse from my hide so as no' to offend our ladies' noses. Shall you escort me to the privy now, to watch me piss?"

"As Domnall sorely worries on you, mayhap I shall." Broden's dark eyes shifted over him. "Fack, you've feathers."

He froze. "Brother, permit me—"

"Oh, aye, *now* you'll admit that your wee screechers again start to molt." The trapper reached out and plucked at his hair, producing one of Dive's tail feathers. "You might have said before." He flicked away the slender quill. "Gods, but they'll be shedding everywhere from now until the first snow."

"As they've done every change of season since we returned from the underworld." Kiaran turned away, and quickly swiped the beads of sweat popping out on his face. "'Tis their nature."

"As you claim every change of season." Broden picked up his discarded tunic and draped it over the chair beside his pallet. "Your lady rides well, mine tells me. Most Pritani females never had cause to oft ride." When Kiaran eyed him he said, "Mariena saw you on patrol from the tower."

"Lilias shall accompany me on patrol, but she isnae mine," he assured him flatly. "She also used no power on me or the mount. She's a sweet, gentle lass, and the mare took to her at once."

"As the lady to you." The trapper folded his arms and leaned back against the wall. "I ken you've cared naught for females, or anyone, but you need unwavering reason to continue the fight. Permit Lilias be that."

He covered his relief with a short laugh. "Aye, as I'm such a prize."

"She doesnae see you as the great scabrous dolt we ken and endure," Broden countered, but his expression softened. "Listen to me now. 'Tis naught in the world as light and joyous as taking a lady wife. You'll discover why when you wake with her in your arms at dawn, and find reason to be very late to the morning meal. Indeed, she'll ever kindle your blood, and burn as the fire in your heart."

"I've facked females," Kiaran reminded him. "No' three tribe's worth as you, but enough. 'Tis a pleasant thing, but no' necessary to me."

"*Pleasant* as 'tis, there's more to having a lady than the facking," the trapper chided mockingly. He sighed and made a gesture over his chest. "Love, real love, changes a man. 'Tis the making of him. You've seen what I've gained since Mariena came back to me. Surely Lilias shall do the same for you."

"Why should she, then?" He couldn't tell his brother why, so he went with the old excuse. "I've but a cold heart to offer her."

"Lilias might have run to any of us, but she chose you," Broden told him, and clapped his hand on his shoulder. "You've but to give her the man she wants, and in time even your heart shall thaw. Now pull on your boots and return to the keepe. The lady will wish to bid you fair night before she seeks her bed."

Kiaran felt the weight of the trapper's hand

atop the hidden strap of his brace, and nodded. He didn't take a deep breath until Broden grinned, turned and departed.

His secret would keep a little while longer, it seemed.

A tendril of cool wind came into his chamber, catching Dive's tail feather from where it had landed. It floated up and twirled in front of his face as if to mock him.

Chapter Nine

GALAN KEPT HIS protective ward in place as he followed Danar into the Sluath-occupied village. Every demon they passed glared at him with hatred and resentment on their ashen faces. He noted how much their physical beauty had dimmed, and the signs of withering that had begun to show on their bodies. He didn't mistake that for weakness. If anything, Iolar and his army of murderous immortals would be even more dangerous now.

The scent of the air changed, and he looked to the north to see black clouds at the edge of the horizon. By tomorrow the storms would sweep over the ridges and give the demons the ability to fly. But would they be strong enough to face the

Mag Raith? Would the tempest last as long as they needed to battle the Pritani?

"You dinnae fare well without your slaves to sustain you," he said to the big demon, who merely grunted as he led him into Iolar's cottage. "You've sent hunters to gather more, but they'll no' help, shall they? For you cannae contain their souls."

"I'll mention to the prince your touching concern for us." Danar went to a table that had been covered with a dark wool blanket. On it sat a bowl filled with black liquid and a funnel fixed to the end of a thick hollow reed. "Drop the ward and take off your robes."

"I won't tell you how to find the Mag Raith until I attain immortality," Galan warned him as he stripped down to his trews. "I ken Iolar wishes me dead, but if you end me, you shall be trapped in the mortal realm forever."

"It almost seems worth it." The demon's copper-colored eyes glittered with amusement as he watched him approach. "Get on the fucking table."

All Galan had done, everything he'd endured, had brought him to this moment. Thanks to the Mag Raith he'd lost his position as headman, his druid powers, and any hope of reincarnation. They'd snatched from him the chance to find the means with which to resurrect his dead mate, Fiana. By their acts against him they had rendered Galan as any other ordinary mortal, doomed to a single life before he met his beloved's fate. If not for his alliance with the Sluath against the Pritani bastarts, even now he would likely be rotting in a grave, as lost to time as Fiana.

He had seen the wonders of immortality transform the facking Mag Raith, and he would have the same for himself. In a few moments he would be as they had become, or be cast into endless oblivion. He wondered if any mortal had ever faced such a test of courage.

"Are you afraid?" the big demon asked as he moved closer.

"You ken the answer to that." Galan perched on the edge before lowering himself so that he lay on his back. "Do the work."

"Any particular place you want me to apply the ink?" Danar asked.

"Here, where all may see." He touched the bones at the base of this throat. "I willnae hide what I become this day."

"How convenient." The big demon drew one

of the blades from his harness. As Galan stiffened he smiled. "Don't worry, little tree-lover. You have to be cut for the magic in the ink to work into your blood."

What followed was a slow, exquisitely agonizing torment. Danar plied the sharp tip of the blade against Galan's flesh, slicing thin yet deep wounds around the bones. Blood ran sluggishly from the cuts over his shoulders. He endured the pain, taking hold of the wool beneath him and bunching it in his fists. At one point he heard the blanket tearing, but he refused to make a sound.

"Well done," Danar said as he wiped clean his dripping blade. "Now where will we find the rebels?"

"I'm no' yet immortal," Galan said through his clenched teeth.

"You will undergo the change after I apply the ink, but that will be far more torturous than this." The demon flicked a claw against the cuts he'd made. "Tell me where they are, and I'll finish the tattoo. You'll get what you deserve, Aedth. On my honor, I swear it."

The lie he had prepared came so easily off his tongue. "The Mag Raith occupy the hills bordering the midlands, twenty leagues to the west. They dwell in the caves of the flat-topped rise overlooking three lochans, hidden by blinds made to resemble rockfalls. The entire place is warded to mask their presence."

"Clever." Danar picked up the bowl of ink. "You're right, we would never have detected them behind a spell barrier."

"You mustnae attack until I've changed," Galan told him, hissing in a breath as a black drop fell into one of his new wounds. "I shall lead you in honor of our prince."

"We'll attack as soon as that storm arrives." A deep, scathing laugh came from the big demon. "For a mortal you are remarkably dense. Why would you believe any Sluath has an ounce of honor?"

Danar flung the ink in Galan's face, blinding him.

The burn of the thick, cold liquid felt like gentle sunlight compared to the terrible slashing that came next as Danar's claws tore through Galan's neck. Pain unlike anything the druid had ever felt filled his head, sinking like white-hot iron into raw flesh. When he tried to scream blood gushed from his mouth.

Feeling his life pulse away in fountaining spurts, Galan sank into darkness, his thoughts ablaze with bitterness and fury. He felt no particular ire toward the demon, for Danar had acted according to his nature. Soon he'd also discover that he had lied about the Mag Raith. But now Galan would never be reunited with Fiana, and having that prize snatched from him made him burn with resentment.

'Tis pleasing to you, my conniving wife, to ken I die for love of you? Mayhap 'twas what you wished for me. My reward after so many centuries and lifetimes of suffering and longing for you. Now I've naught, and 'twas all your doing.

Eternity came and went as oblivion kept Galan enveloped by its cavernous maw. Release came in piercing shafts of new pain that rammed through every part of his body. Swords of molten agony hacked at his hands and his back and his face. The hatred in him swelled, as ravenous as a starving hog, and pushed him to the brink of madness, and then over the edge. He fell endlessly into the darkness, his limbs now as numb as if turned to lead, and landed in wet, stinking carrion.

Was this the underworld? Had Danar pushed

him through a gate after he'd torn out his throat? Why did the air buzz in his ears? What now skittered over his frozen flesh?

After a miserable eternity of torment Galan felt the pain begin to retreat. Although his body still felt as if frozen, when he reached for his throat his arm moved, and his heavy hand clamped around his slick neck. Why did his fingers feel as if they'd grown long and curving? He felt the edges of the terrible wound closing, and opened his blurry eyes.

Above him sat a perfect circle of star-spangled black, across which moonlit streams of clouds moved. All around that sphere of night sky fell rough walls with spiky shadows that moved in the flickering light of a torch. Galan turned his head to see the silhouette of a skull. Danar had dropped him into the charnel pit the Sluath had been using as a mass grave.

You'll get what you deserve, Aedth.

Pushing himself up from the mound of corpses beneath him, Galan planted his hand against one side of the pit, and saw why his fingers felt as they did. He had sprouted claws like one of the demons. Then his back bowed and the wings Iolar had grafted onto his back spread out on either side of him. His scarlet and white feathers had all turned to a silver-edged onyx.

He had become immortal—an immortal Sluath.

Using his new claws, Galan crawled up the wall of the pit, gouging out huge handfuls of soil as he tested the strength of his transformed limbs. At the top he hoisted himself out and stood, his wings folding neatly against his back as he looked down at the village. Most of the Sluath had retreated for the night, but he spied some demons dragging a pair of struggling mortal females toward Iolar's cottage.

Unfamiliar potency swelled inside him as he pulled the standing torch from the ground, adding to the stores of magic Iolar had given him.

"Hungry, my prince?" Galan sent a little of his new power into the shaft of the torch, and murmured a spell. That divided the torch's flames into dozens of blazing spheres that floated out around him, hovering in the dark air. "Mayhap first I should cook your meal—and you."

He rammed more power into the spheres before he flung them at the village. When they slammed into the rooftops, flames devoured the dry-rotted thatching and rained down on the insides of the cottages. Listening to the distant, shrill screams of the demons gave Galan his first taste of pleasure as an immortal. He wanted to linger and watch them all burn, but he needed to be closer to the Mag Raith when the storm arrived.

Smiling as he cloaked himself in shadow, he turned away from the pyre of demons and headed for the trail that would take him to his mount tethered in the trees, and his final act of vengeance.

Chapter Ten

WHEN KIARAN RETURNED to the stronghold only Domnall occupied the great hall, where he sat studying a scroll by candlelight. The other man's expression, unguarded for once, appeared bleak. He hesitated, unsure if he should disturb him at such a moment, but the chieftain would be expecting a report on the day's events.

What troubles him?

Kiaran rarely gave any thought to the unseen burdens the chieftain carried on his shoulders. The weight of his responsibilities to the clan and his lady wife never left him. Under threat of Sluath attack they'd doubtless grown crushing. Against an army of demons, he had four hunters and five females. Of the ladies, only Mariena possessed true skill with weapons and fighting. To protect them they had but a crumbling castle filled with traps created by a mad immortal who also wished them all dead.

For the first time Kiaran saw just how truly desperate their predicament was. *'Twill be a miracle if we prevail.*

"Dinnae hover like your hunters," Domnall said as he rolled up the parchment and set it aside. "The ladies have retired for the night, so you've no more to do." He rubbed his eyes before he regarded him. "By the Gods. You look as I feel."

"I'll endure." He joined him and reported on the day's events, finishing with, "We saw no sign of the demons at the barrier, nor in any direction away from the keepe."

"We? You patrolled with the lass?" When he nodded the chieftain grunted. "She said naught of her day with you, yet I saw no sign of any discomfort when she left the hall."

"She rides as well as any of us." He described Lilias's ease with handling the mare before he said, "I'll keep patrolling with her, if I may, while you and the others see to the work within the keepe."

"Aye, 'twould aid us greatly." Domnall rose to his feet. "Kiaran, I'd ask your pardon for this morning, in the forge." As he started to shake his head the chieftain raised one hand. "No' for what I said to you. I meant every word. I shouldnae have spoken to you in such a dark mood." He offered his hand. "Forgive me, Brother."

All of the sympathy Kiaran felt evaporated, and the fierce urge to plow his fist into the other man's jaw made him take a step back. Despite many misgivings he'd been steadfast and loyal to Domnall since they'd begun hunting together in their mortal lives. He'd tried his best to protect the clan, only to be viewed as a traitor and outsider. He'd never be to the Mag Raith what they were to each other. Forever he would be left outside, watching and wanting but never having their kinship.

A flash of Lilias's gilded eyes burned through his ire. *Dinnae give him reason to drive you from Dun Chaill, and her.*

"If you'll offer me the same mercy." With a stiff smile Kiaran clasped forearms with him. "I shouldnae prod your moods to darkness so often."

"Jenna claims in the future 'tis something called 'anger management' they compel the short-tempered to learn." One side of Domnall's mouth hitched. "Yet another reason I'm content to remain in this time. Until the morrow, Brother."

Kiaran kept his pleasant expression plastered on his face as he left the stronghold, and stalked back to his tower. He could feel more than one gaze on his back, and suspected both Broden and Mariena watched him from some hidden spot. Likely on Domnall's orders. The chieftain no longer trusted him, and likely never would again.

When he reached the tower, Sift fluttered in front of him, but darted up again. His simmering wrath made him snatch at the bird, catching it in his fist. The kestrel went still, and gazed at his master with a familiar glow in his dark eyes. The sense of absolute trust that came through their connection melted away Kiaran's fury. The bird did not fight his hold because, like the other kestrels, he believed the falconer would never harm him.

When he released Sift the raptor simply moved to perch on his wrist.

"Forgive me." As he smoothed down the wing and tail feathers he'd ruffled on the kestrel's small body, he thought of his reaction to Domnall's attempt to reconcile with him. In the past such a thing would never have made him angry. "I'm no' myself this night."

Knowing he would not sleep, Kiaran tidied his chamber, pulled on his work gloves, and then climbed the new stairs he'd built in the tower. Above his own retreat he'd begun installing long perches and inset platforms to create an aviary. He needed something to do other than pace until dawn, and his raptors would need shelter from the snow and wind during the winter months.

Some hours later he stopped and surveyed the last of the iron and wood supports he'd fixed to the stone work. It felt good to work, and made him feel stronger and clearer in his thoughts. He'd spent too much time worrying on what might be, and not attending to what was.

A shift of shadows through the window slit across from him drew his attention. He approached the narrow opening, and through it saw Lilias carrying a basket out of the kitchens garden. She stopped and looked up at the stronghold, but made no move to return inside. Tucking his mallet in his belt, he hurried down and out of the tower.

"My lady." He saw the surprise on her face as she saw him. "What do you outside at this hour?"

"Fair night, Kiaran." Lilias ducked her head. "Sleep eludes me, so I thought I'd walk the grounds. Sitting in the dark with naught to do, 'tis maddening."

Hot blood rushed to his hardening cock as he imagined how tired she'd be after the many pleasures he could give her, had he still been a man.

Dinnae think of her thus, for you'll no' have her.

"'Tis too dark to go walking."

Her gaze shifted past him for a moment. "I didnae intend to go far."

Kiaran glanced down at the basket in her hand, which she'd filled with strawberries. "You neednae gather food, you ken. Lady Rosealise keeps our pantry well-stocked."

"'Tis hard to resist them. They smell as pleasing as they taste." She glanced past him again, and he realized she was looking at the tower. "What do you in there?"

The right thing to do would be escorting her back to her chamber, but he hated the thought of her all alone in the dark. Even if it made him a selfish bastart, he also wanted more time with her. "Come and I'll show you."

Lilias walked with him through the gap that led into the ruined tower. As he tugged aside the old tartan she set down her basket and studied his makeshift chamber.

He suddenly realized how rough it must look compared to the stronghold. "'Tisnae so grand, but I crave quiet, no' comforts."

"'Tis peaceful here." Lilias glanced up. "Do you build another chamber now?"

"Of sorts, but no' for me." He gestured to the stairs, and followed her up into the aviary. The torch he'd left burning flickered light over the fixtures and the kestrels that now occupied them.

Lilias halted as soon as she saw the birds, and took a step back.

"They willnae harm you," he assured her. "As a lad I tamed them, and taught them to hunt with me." He beckoned to Dive, who flew down to perch on his wrist.

The kestrel locked gazes with her, and both beheld each other as if unsure of what to think.

"The wee lady here I named Dive. She's the first I tamed." He might as well tell her all. "'Tis my power to command her and all the kestrels. I ken their thoughts, and may see through their eyes."

She looked perplexed now. "You cannae do the same with other birds?"

"Most fear me and mine." He tapped the end of Dive's beak. "When first we brought the poultry to Dun Chaill, my kestrels thought them prey. I saved most, but the survivors havenae forgot."

"Ah." Lilias nodded. "The chickens hold a grudge, then."

Dive chose that moment to utter a low trill, and flew from Kiaran's wrist to Lilias's shoulder. She preened for a moment before rubbing the top of her head against the side of the Pritani woman's jaw in a very rare show of affection.

Kiaran grinned. "'Twould seem my small lady finds favor with you. Here, you may show yours just so." He took hold of Lilias's hand, and guided her fingers to the kestrel's neck to show her how to gently scratch around the short feathers.

Dive released more trills of pleasure, but as Kiaran felt the other birds' desire to join her, he sent the female back to her perch.

"'Tis best, else you'll soon wear them all," he told Lilias.

"I'd no' mind such a lovely garment." Her head tipped back as she gazed up at the flight. "They're your own wee clan, arenae they?"

His smile faded. "Raiders killed my *máthair*

and her tribe." That much, at least, was truth. "I've no one and naught."

"'Tis the same for me." She sighed. "Worse, I reckon, for I've no' even a name to call myself."

He touched her cheek, which felt cool and smooth against his hard flesh. "You've a kind heart, and such beauty and grace, 'tis almost painful to look upon you."

"Now I ken why Dive does thus." Lilias closed her eyes and rubbed her face against his hand.

Somehow she came into his arms, although Kiaran couldn't tell if he tugged her against him or she stepped closer. Never had a woman felt as right as this. She fit in his embrace so perfectly she might have been carved from his very flesh. Her scent rose between them, soft and cool and fragrant as her namesake. Gods, but he wished he could smother himself in her.

She likely thought all he did unseemly, yet she made no move to pull away. How could he release her when Lilias made him feel as if he'd found some lost part of himself?

"My lady."

Kiaran bent his head to touch his brow to hers, but she lifted her face at the same moment.

As their lips met in a single, perfect kiss, the wild honeyed taste of her filled his head.

She might look the goddess, but the earthy lushness of her filled him with hard, hungry heat.

Distantly Kiaran felt all of the kestrels take to wing, and heard them trilling to each other as they flew from the tower. But feeling the soft silk of Lilias's lips soon swept away every thought but that of her.

"Kiaran." The whisper of his name burst against his mouth. "Ken you me?"

"I shall." He ended the kiss and put his brow to hers, and felt her inked hand touch his arm. Abruptly the tower darkened and shrank around them. *"Lilias."*

KIARAN KEPT his blade ready as he watched the other hunters trot through the stone passage ahead of him. All five of his kestrels clung to his shoulders and head, but he barely felt their weight. He kept checking over his shoulder, but saw no one pursuing them. Broden had sworn he'd seen invaders marching toward the fortress, which had compelled them to hide in the tunnel Edane had found beneath it.

Mael carried the archer's limp body over his broad shoulder. Since clutching his chest and collapsing, Edane had gone as white as bone, and now barely breathed. "Look here, 'tis an entry to another passage."

The hunters stopped before the large arch, which had no door or barrier. Strange symbols had been carved in the stone on every side of it. More had been etched into the floor. Beyond it they could see nothing. Even the light from their torches did not penetrate the blackness inside the curved opening.

"'Tis a pit trap," Broden predicted darkly, his ruined voice barely above a whisper.

"Even if Edane could be moved, we cannae flee on foot in the storm," Domnall told him. "I'll go first."

"No, together," Kiaran said, suspecting why the Romans had marched on the fortress: the Mag Raith headman had lied to him. Whatever they did, they were all dead men anyway, and this time he would not run from it. "If 'tis a facking stake-filled hole, then we die as one. As brothers."

Broden muttered a curse, but nodded along with Mael.

Domnall searched their faces before he smiled a little. "As brothers."

The four of them ducked through the arch, which crackled with white-blue light as they did. Kiaran felt it glance off his flesh and saw it do the same to the others, and felt a strange coldness rising inside him. On the other side was not a pit trap or utter darkness, but more passages hewn through the stone.

All of the hunters held their blades ready, even Mael.

Kiaran looked down at himself. The light cast by the arch had danced over his skin, but now slid down his chest and limbs as if water. It sank into the rock under his boots before it disappeared.

"'Tis somehow enchanted," Domnall said as he scanned the tunnels, his mouth tight. He sniffed the air. "Another watches us."

"One of those facking druids, hoping to snare Romans," Broden said, and gestured back toward the arch. "We're caught."

Kiaran turned to see the entry had vanished along with the light.

"Aye, but Edane's breathing better now." Mael

carefully lowered the archer down onto the stone. "Lad, can ye open yer eyes?"

Kiaran's kestrels dug their talons into him, and when he listened hard he heard what alarmed them. "Dinnae try to rouse him."

"Why no', Kiaran?" Mael asked.

"Listen." His eyes abruptly darkened as he nodded past them. "They come for us."

Something on the other side of the passage moved then, and Kiaran saw a small, huddled figure watching them. The moment he saw the fear in her golden-brown eyes he recognized it, for he had seen the same every day of his boyhood in his mother's.

He strode over to her, taking her by the arms and pulling her to her feet. The cloak she wore disguised much of her, but the manacles around her thin wrists and ankles told him what she could not hide.

"Ye're a slave here, lass?"

"Aye." Her throat moved as she swallowed. "You…you must come with me now."

Her strange way of speaking unsettled him almost as much as her eyes.

"I cannae leave them." Kiaran swung back toward the other hunters to call to them, and then felt her cold hand clutching his arm. "Dinnae fear. Come with me, and we'll take ye with us back through the arch."

With surprising strength, the lass jerked him back into the shadows, where a dark blue light flared across the stone wall. A moment later he stood in another place, as if she had pulled him through the very stone itself. Through a panel of clear ice, he saw dozens of stunning, god-like creatures surrounding the other hunters. With tremendous strength and speed, they disarmed the three left standing, and knocked them to the ground before chaining them together with Edane and dragging them away.

"The others may tell the guards of you," she whispered to him as they both stood. "I cannae return you to your world, but I shall hide you."

"What of my brothers?" Although on one level Kiaran knew what he saw was a vision, the words still came from him hot with anger. "We must go after them and end those facking things that took them."

"We cannae fight them, Warrior." She stiffened at the sound of approaching footsteps, and took hold of his hand. "Come, now, or you shall be made a slave as well."

He followed her through the tunnels to an alcove, where she pressed her hand against two marks. A large arch appeared in the stone, through which she tugged him. As soon as they stood inside the chamber within, the opening solidified back into rock.

His kestrels huddled close to him, silent with terror now.

Light flared around them, revealing a small bed chamber containing bizarre furnishings made of white stone. Kiaran turned around, bewildered by the strangeness of the blue flames burning in tall glass braziers, from which he felt no heat nor smelled any scent. Rough, stained linen garments hung next to incredibly colored, finely-embroidered gowns. An oval of silver reflected his face so perfectly he might have been looking at a twin.

"Where bring ye me?" he demanded.

Lilias removed the shackles from her wrists and ankles and placed them on a table that looked carved from ice. "'Tis my chamber. 'Twas where my *máthair* birthed me in secret and hid me."

Kiaran peered at her. "Why did she thus?"

"The Sluath enslaved her," Lilias told him as she sat down on a wide, silk-covered divan. "The king of this underworld took many breeding females from your world. She saw that he never learned of me."

He felt sickened. "She left ye locked in this chamber?"

"After she stopped chaining me I didnae mind so much." She saw his expression. "'Twasnae that my *máthair* meant to be cruel. She worried I might wander away when I was a little one. She came to see me as often as she could, and taught me much. The king wouldnae have been so kind."

Nothing she said made sense to him, but he went to her, and drew her to her feet. "Take me to my brothers."

"'Tis naught you may do for them." Lilias gripped his hands tightly. "Even now they change."

Kiaran pushed her against the wall and held her there, causing the kestrels to take to their wings and scatter. "What mean ye, change?"

"Forgive me," Lilias said, and touched his cheek.

Chapter Eleven

MORNING LIGHT STREAMING through the old tartan curtain roused Kiaran from the shadowy dregs of oblivion. His head ached miserably, and beneath him his back throbbed in kind beneath the brace. When he sat up he saw he'd taken to his pallet while still wearing his trews and tunic. For a moment he wondered if he'd merely dreamed the interlude with Lilias. He wanted her so much he might have convinced himself of the kiss and the strange vision that had overtaken him. Then he saw his boots by the hearth, where a banked fire still glowed.

I never sought my bed.

His habit as a defender for the Moss Dapple tribe had always been to put his boots within reach so he might quickly don them. Domnall had taught him that as a precaution, in the event an attack came during the night. If he'd taken them off, he'd never put them anywhere else. While he did sleep with his brace on, in hopes of stunting the growth of his wings, he always quenched the hearth before seeking his bed. The drafts that came through the tower at night could fling embers about and start a fire.

So, it seemed the kiss and the vision had been real. The shock of what he had seen must have knocked him out. But how had Lilias put him to bed? He'd never match Domnall or Mael for size, but he wasn't a small man, either. She could not have carried him down from the aviary to put him to bed.

Had she dragged him?

Determined to get answers, Kiaran yanked on his boots before he started for the stronghold. Halfway there Nellie stepped into his path, bringing him to a halt.

"Catching up on your beauty sleep, Bird Man?" the petite American asked, her dislike of him sharpening the words. "Or are you just turning into a self-pitying lay about?"

"I need speak with Lilias." He tried to go around her, but she moved quickly to counter that. "You wish something more from me than strips of my hide, my lady?"

"Golly, the list I could make. But that can wait for Santa." Nellie shifted to stand beside him and gestured toward the barn. "Come into my office. We need to chat about Lilias."

Kiaran held onto his temper as he accompanied her inside, where she closed the doors and regarded him without a glimmer of glee. "Domnall ordered me return to the stronghold and look after the newcomer. 'Twasnae my notion or desire. Now may I go?"

"Again, not about you." She circled around him and leaned against one of the stanchions where a spotted heifer nuzzled her arm. "Behave, Boopsey. After this I'll put a warm compress on that blocked teat and we'll get you going again. Where was I? Oh, yeah. I stood watch last night. Seems that Pritani gal likes to sneak out to go strawberry picking by her lonesome. So, you stink at looking after her."

For the harm he'd done to Nellie, Kiaran

would accept her retaliation in kind. He deserved it. But he wouldn't allow her to use an innocent lass as a weapon against him.

"How the lady spends her nights, 'tis naught to do with me."

"Really." Nellie stroked the cow's head. "Lilias also likes tip-toeing out of your little tower hold-up. You know, alone, near dawn, looking guilty, not that you'd know anything about that, either, huh?"

The American seemed determined to see the worst in everyone. "She's but a simple Pritani lass—"

"Who was locked up with me in the underworld for maybe a hundred years. Decked in pretty duds and jewels and guarded like a demon princess. I touch-read her pendant," Nellie added before he could reply. "Lilias was Prince Iolar's greatest treasure. You remember, the one he tried to kill us all to get back because he thought I stole it? And I don't think it's only because she's such a Sheba. The whole clan thinks she's the cat's pajamas. Even you, and you only like your lady birds."

Everything she'd said hit Kiaran like a cudgel to the chest. "Fack me."

"I'd bed a demon first," she assured him,

smiling with soft malice. "But, like I said, not about you. I want to know what sweet, gentle Lilias is doing to the clan. So, spill. What happened between you two last night?"

"We but talked," he said quickly. "She fell asleep, and I gave her my bed and slept by the hearth."

"You used to be such a swell liar. What happened?" When he said nothing, she wriggled her fingers. "Don't make me read it from your rags."

If she did, she'd find out more than Kiaran wanted her or the clan to know, which decided the matter for him. "I showed to Lilias the aviary I've built for the kestrels. We embraced, and…mayhap we shared a vision."

Once he described what he'd seen, Nellie straightened. "Come on. Jenna and Domnall are working in the forge this morning. You need to tell them what you remembered right now."

"If 'twas real." Kiaran put a hand on the barn door to keep it closed. "The traitor among the demons meddled with Mariena's memories. Mayhap he did the same to mine."

"Well, you can tell them that, too." She

regarded him and made an impatient sound. "Kiaran, if the Sluath didn't cull you guys, it changes the whole story."

"No' for the better," he warned.

Nellie folded her arms. "Say, I know all about pretty lies. I buried myself inside a big one, see? The truth may be ugly, but facing it, we can do better."

Kiaran's back brace seemed to grow tighter. "Aye."

He went with Nellie through the back of the stronghold to access the side entry to the forge. They found the chieftain and his mate with a bundle of old iron swords collected from the hoard mound.

"We brought these to be reworked as crossbow bolts," Domnall said, cutting the cord around the bundle, and then frowned at Nellie. "Need you help seeing to the stock?" When she shook her head, he regarded Kiaran. "You surely dinnae need the lady plying a sledge."

"Lilias came to me in the night, and I think mayhap we shared a vision." Kiaran related what had happened, and all the details of what he had seen. "If 'tis a memory in truth, then 'twas no' as we've ever reckoned. We found our way into the underworld through an opened gate. 'Twas beneath the old fortress, at the end of a passage hewn through stone. I saw many more leading in other directions. 'Twas as a warren."

"Tunnels below ground," Domnall muttered. "Yet we've seen no sign of any since returning here."

Jenna's eyes widened. "Maybe we weren't supposed to find them. We know the watcher uses magic to conceal his arches and traps inside the castle. He probably used warding spells to keep us from finding the tunnels as well as where he gains access to them."

"Stone would quiet any sound he makes," Kiaran said. "'Tis likely he's bespelled entry ways to every part of Dun Chaill."

"Swell." Nellie rubbed her brow. "He's operating his own private speakeasy, right under our feet." She eyed Kiaran. "Tell them the rest."

"We dinnae ken 'tis a power," he said, glaring at her, "but Lady Nellie brought up how wholly and quickly the clan comes to favor the lass. 'Twas the same with the mare I gave her to ride, and my kestrels."

"You believe she has the power to…what? Bewitch everyone?" Jenna asked, sounding skeptical.

Domnall eyed Kiaran. "Or she may have some manner of seduction power."

"I think it's something nicer than that," Nellie said, "or we'd all be trying to jump in the sack with the gal. It's more like she somehow makes us all feel good when she's around, really good. We like her, we trust her, and we say nice things about her. But Jenny, she just got here. Remember how we treated Mariena when she woke up?"

"Lilias didn't take a blade to Kiaran's throat," the chieftain's wife said, frowning. "She would never hurt anyone, she's really gentle and sweet."

"That's it. We all say that about her, in those exact words," Nellie said. "Even I've said them."

"Ladies, mayhap you'd do me the favor of summoning Edane, Broden and Mael to the forge, that we may tell them what we now ken," Domnall said. Once the women had left he eyed Kiaran. "Whatever power Lilias possesses, 'tisnae what concerns me most. You're certain that the Mag Raith walked through the Sluath gate. The same manner of gate that 'twould end any mortal that attempted thus from either side. If 'tis truth, this vision of yours—"

Kiaran nodded. "When we found the underworld, we werenae mortal." He glanced over at the fortifications he'd been forging for their defense. "And Lilias, she's no' what she seems."

Chapter Twelve

⚜

GATHERING THE COURAGE to leave her chamber took Lilias most of the morning, as she expected Kiaran to come and collect her. He would have questions that she couldn't answer, unless the shock of the vision had been too much for him. Perhaps he wouldn't recall anything, or assume he'd dreamt what he did. She'd been so unnerved by his embrace that, after it, she'd forgotten everything but sitting and watching him in wonder as he slept.

She felt certain that he'd retained no memory of her before he'd taken her into his arms. To him, everything about her was strange and new and unfamiliar, and still… She shook her head.

'Twas my beauty that drew him to me, no' his heart.

Knowing she would soon drive herself mad with such thoughts, Lilias donned the tunic and trousers Jenna had given her. Her fingers shook as she tried to braid her hair, failed and left it hanging on her shoulders. She couldn't help peeking into the passage before stepping out and walking toward the great hall. There she saw the trestle table and its benches hanging on the wall, and felt a twinge of relief. Soon she'd have to share meals with the others, but she needed more time to watch the clan and learn.

"Fair morning, Lilias," Rosealise called from the kitchens. "Come and join me. I've saved some pottage and bread for your morning meal."

As soon as she joined the housekeeper Lilias offered her the strawberries.

"I picked these last night. I didnae ken you've food stored." As Rosealise took the basket she added, "When their fragrance came to me, I couldnae help myself."

"Please don't concern yourself, my dear. We can never have too many berries." The housekeeper placed the basket on her work table, and brought back a tray with a bowl, sliced bread and a small pot. "Here, you must be hungry."

Lilias eyed the two instruments beside the bowl. One resembled a blade and had a rounded tip, but the other looked like a miniature bowl on a handle. She wasn't sure if she was to drink from the larger bowl, which had chunks of veg in the steaming liquid.

"I much prefer the simple table settings of this era. Far less trouble than the dozen pieces of cutlery required at every meal in my time." Rosealise sat down across from her with the exact same meal she'd given her, and held up the tiny handled bowl. "This, for example, is a spoon for eating the pottage, porridge, stew or any sort of liquid dish. When I came here I had no idea the utensils would prove so versatile."

Lilias watched as she dipped the curved end into the bowl and brought a small amount from it to her lips. Carefully she did the same.

Rosealise then held up the strange blade. "Jam knife." She opened the pot and used the end of the knife to remove a dollop of gleaming dark substance, which she spread on the bread slice. "It also serves to spread butter, cream, paté, preserves and all manner of soft foods eaten on bread or oatcakes. That is also why the edges are blunted, so you should not attempt to cut anything with it."

"Oh." That the housekeeper had noticed her ignorance made Lilias cringe a little. "My thanks."

As they ate together Rosealise talked about making the jam from blackberries mixed with honey, and how she'd do the same with the basket of strawberries. Lilias silently marveled at how the other woman seemed more worried about preserving fruit than the coming attack.

"I remember my father describing the weather in Scotland," Rosealise mentioned as she rose to clear their dishes. "He claimed the month of June would be lovely and warm, followed by eleven months of storms. I thought he exaggerated, but my dear Mael assures me that we may expect a great deal of snow this winter."

"Snow." As she went to help her, Lilias tried to imagine everything covered by mounds of white ice. "I dinnae ken how 'twill be."

"Quite cold. I daresay we shall be very grateful for our woolens when the winter arrives." The housekeeper handed her a clean cloth and a wet bowl to dry. "I'm sure Jenna told you about the gifts the demons bestowed on us."

"Aye." She looked through the window at the herb garden, which looked so pretty in the sunlight that she sighed. "'Tis a great boon for the clan to have such powers."

"Most of the time they are, although they can be troubling as well. My own is a compulsion ability. When I touch someone, they must do my bidding. I can even force them to tell the truth." Rosealise emptied the bin of washing water and untied her apron. "It has become more than it was in the beginning. Lately, whenever someone lies to me, I feel a very strong yearning to touch them, presumably to use my gift on them."

Lilias joined her and met her gaze. "I havenae lied to you."

"All I feel when I am near you is complete contentment and delight, as I would with a good and trusted friend." The housekeeper smiled. "I hope that we may enjoy such concord someday, for you seem to me a very agreeable young woman. Truly I've never met anyone as gentle or sweet. As we are veritable strangers, however, for me to feel such warmth toward you is highly suspect."

"Use your compulsion on me, then." When the housekeeper didn't touch her, she took hold of Rosealise's hands. "I'd earn your trust, my lady. Ask, please, what wish you to ken of me."

"As long as you're willing, very well." Her gentle gray eyes darkened. "Tell me, my dear, what is your name?"

She felt the other woman's power radiating from her like the heat from a hearth. "Lilias."

Surprise flickered over Rosealise's pretty features. "Do you remember the name you were given at birth?"

That she genuinely wished she could answer differently. "No, my lady."

Compassion softened the other woman's gaze. "Do you know why you came to Dun Chaill?"

"Aye." Holding hands with Rosealise allowed her to feel the lovely warmth of the housekeeper's touch. "Here I willnae be enslaved, or tormented, or made to hide. Among your clan I may live as one of you: free."

"My dear, we want that for you as well, but we must be sure of your intentions." Rosealise's fingers tightened. "Is there something you are concealing from us?"

Before she could answer the housekeeper's gaze shifted, and the scent of a chilly wind wafted between them. She abruptly released Lilias's hands.

"My dear sir, please don't be angry," Rosealise

said, her cheeks reddening. "The young lady requested that I use my ability on her."

Lilias turned to see Kiaran scowling at them.

"'Tis truth. I wish to ken more." She reached for Rosealise's hands, but the housekeeper moved out of reach.

"'Twill wait for another time, my ladies," he said, his tone flinty. "Come, Lilias. We must patrol now."

Chapter Thirteen

BY THE TIME he rode past the burnt ruins of Wachvale, Galan felt the air cool, and saw the shadows around him stretching longer. The approaching storm had billowed up beyond the ridges, and would soon swallow the sun. The looming tempest strangely invigorated him, and each time distant lightning flashed he felt power throb in his core. He longed to soar up into the black clouds and roll with the rumbles of thunder. He wanted to glide over the land to hunt something small and helpless and mortal.

Yet before he could indulge his new Sluath abilities and appetites, he had to seek recompense for all he'd suffered at the hands of the Mag Raith.

"Aye, they shall suffer," Galan murmured as he looked past the charred remains of his past toward the hidden castle. "All that I've endured and more."

He had already discarded the idea of cloaking himself in the guise of an ordinary mortal before attempting to again invade Dun Chaill. Anyone seen approaching the ruined castle would be viewed as a threat by the watchful clan. Even with his new immortal powers he could not take on all five Pritani at once and hope to survive. In order to slaughter the hunters, he would have to turn their tactics against them to get them alone where he could attack each one without warning. To isolate the men, he'd use a lure so irresistible they would run to their deaths at his hands.

Their love for their precious mates would be their undoing.

Once he'd taken the heads of each and every Mag Raith, Galan would go and collect their sluts. The females from the future wouldn't stand a chance against his might. Jenna Cameron would be the first he'd defile. He could almost hear her screams for mercy now.

Perhaps he'd keep Domnall alive long enough to watch his wife's torment.

Galan crossed the glen, and returned to the spot where he had first passed through the spell barrier. There he dismounted to retrieve the body of the mortal spy he'd killed. The smell of his rotting flesh reminded him of his awakening to immortality in the charnel pit, but the stench no longer disgusted him. Soon this would be all that remained of the Mag Raith.

"You shall provide one last service to me," he told the dead man. Adequately draping himself required some tearing apart and rearranging of the flesh, but at last he hefted the torn corpse up and settled the remains over his head, shoulders and arms. "Ha. The prince spoke truth. 'Tis possible to make a human into a garment."

His horse uttered a squeal and skittered away.

As he approached the barrier, Galan felt the Pritani magic used to construct it like so many tiny claws in the air. Whatever he had been before climbing out of the pit had truly died, and it gladdened him. Never again would he have to live as a mewling, impotent mortal, or be reborn to again endure the aging process. Once he finished the

Mag Raith, he would hunt Culvar and force him to reopen the gates to his new kingdom.

All the Sluath slaves waiting in the underworld would be his to enjoy.

Galan hesitated before he stepped into the shimmering boundary, but grew furious with himself. What did he have to fear? Even if his passage forewarned the halfling, what could Culvar do to stop him?

He stepped into the barrier, and the magic parted around the dead flesh. A moment later he felt it close again behind him, undisturbed.

Once he had uncloaked, he carried the mortal's torn body deep into the forest between the river and the castle, where he climbed a tall birch. His claws made his ascent as easy as walking across a glen. Wedging the corpse securely in the top branches where it would not be spotted, he dropped back down to the ground and listened. The only sound that came from Dun Chaill was the lowing of cattle, and the answering bleat of sheep.

'Tis time to see to the butchering.

Galan moved silently through the trees to circle around to the back of the stronghold, where he followed a well-worn trail. It led to the hoard mound he'd spied on his first visit. The sound of horses approaching made him move to the opposite side of the forest, where he scaled an oak and tugged several branches together to form a blind.

"Now come to me, Mag Raith," he muttered.

He felt surprised by a flare of cold heat at the base of his throat, one that burned through the ever-present longing to feel cringing flesh in his claws. His eyes narrowed as the rider appeared on the trail. Kiaran appeared as stony-faced as ever, but another followed him. Since the second rider looked too slender to be one of the hunters, doubtless he'd brought one of the sluts along.

Galan went still as soon as he saw the female's lovely face, framed by silky dark red hair. Sunlight poured over her, flashing along the garnet strands and warming the new honey color of her flesh. He felt his eyes burn as he stared at what surely had to be the most perfect, flawless features of any creature to ever walk the earth.

Fiana.

He knew her better than himself. He had dreamed of her again and again in every one of his incarnations. He had loved her beyond anything, even reason. He had watched her die after giving birth to his loathsome son. Yet here she was, as stunning and vibrant as she had been when they had mated.

Here, at Dun Chaill, with Kiaran mag Raith.

Chapter Fourteen

KIARAN SAID NOTHING to Lilias until they rode from the stables along the forest trail, which gave her time to consider what to tell him. Even if she'd wished to, she couldn't have lied to Rosealise. She loved being free and having the chance to live the life she should have had as a Pritani woman. At the same time, she felt glad she hadn't answered that last question.

'Tisnae time yet.

Last night had proven without uncertainty that she could have what she most wanted: Kiaran and freedom. She had to be patient but a little while longer, and continue proving herself to the Mag Raith. That would assure that the clan accepted her as one of their own, and then she could uncover all that yet remained hidden.

Kiaran rode through the forest, slowing his pace as the trees thinned. Lilias saw beyond them a pass between the slopes with a very old trail, one she could barely make out. A far-off fall of water sparkled as it came down the rugged stones, and swelled into the river that bordered the stronghold. High above their heads she noticed the kestrels hovering, and wondered why they kept their distance. Perhaps it had to do with the change in his scent, which seemed to grow colder now as he regarded her with a flinty gaze.

"I woke to find myself in my bed," he said, startling her. "I've no memory of how I landed in it, but 'twould seem you put me there."

"I couldnae wake you, so I helped you to bed, and sat with you," Lilias told him quickly. "I reckoned I shouldnae leave you alone thus."

Kiaran reined in his gelding, turning the horse so that it blocked the trail. "Yet you left just after dawn. Edane's mate Nellie saw you creep from the tower."

He spoke as if he were accusing her of some offense, but then she was already lying to him. "I reckoned the others would soon awake, and 'twas proper I no' be found alone with you. That your clan might think me unseemly."

The short laugh he uttered sounded bitter. "My clan's too busy with their bedplay to care what we do, my lady." He swung down from the gelding and came to hold up his arms. "We shall walk from here."

Walk to where? As she dismounted with his help, all she could see was the ancient forest, and the faint shimmer of the enchanted barrier at its edge. Once he'd tethered the horses she accompanied him through a thicket of pine. On the other side of it rose an enormous mound of mossy earth. Partly covered on one side by a row of large wooden panels, it looked like a small hill.

"'Tis the hoard Jenna spoke of?" she asked, bewildered now.

"Aye." Kiaran went to pull aside the center panel, revealing the hollow behind it. "We've dug out this side so we might take what we need."

She went to stand beside him, but as soon as she saw the pile of ancient swords she stepped back. "Why bring me here?"

"To show you the hoard. 'Tis all that remains of the mortals Culvar, the watcher, killed here. We reckon he slaughtered any mortal who strayed too near Dun Chaill." He reached in and extracted a bundle of short, rusted swords. "Roman blades." He tossed it aside and removed a strangely-carved, rotted wooden club. "Druid cudgel." That he threw down by the blade before he dragged out a pair of bronze-tipped rods gone green with moss. "Pritani spears."

The splintering sounds the ancient lances made as he dropped them atop the other weapons made her flinch, but the sudden chill in the air frightened her more.

"The watcher didnae need mortal weapons, for 'tis killing magic he uses." Kiaran turned toward her, his dark eyes ablaze with fury. "Spells to bewitch and trap and end the unwary. 'Tis sickening, for the unwary couldnae ever fight against such."

Somehow she had to calm him. "I dinnae ken your meaning."

"You wield the same weapon as the watcher," he told her flatly. "'Tis what you've worked on me and my clan, to force us to care for you."

The shock of his accusation made her glance down at herself, but nothing was amiss with her appearance. "I dinnae possess such magic. Had I such spells, you couldnae be angry with me."

Kiaran shook his head. "Even as I shout at you, I feel tenderness. I wish to care for you, protect you, aye, and keep you. Yet 'tisnae my true desire, Lilias. I've been a cold-hearted bastart all my life, caring for naught but myself."

"Mayhap you wished yourself such a heart." Slowly she walked to him, until only a hand's breadth of space separated them. "In the memory we shared last night you werenae so cold nor selfish. The moment we met, you saw I'd been enslaved. You wished to help *me* escape as well as your brothers."

The chill in the air slowly ebbed as Kiaran looked down at her.

"No female should be kept in chains." The harsh lines around his nose and mouth deepened for a moment before his expression gentled. "Mayhap 'tis a power you possess, to endear yourself to others, but you ken naught of it. Rosealise didnae learn of hers until after Mael realized she'd been compelling him and the clan."

"Have her ask me, then, when we return to the castle." It might force her to reveal more than Lilias wished, but perhaps the time to unveil had arrived.

Kiaran nodded, and walked with her back to

where they'd left the horses. As she reached for the mare's reins he caught her hand in his. "Forgive me. I didnae intend to frighten you."

"I'm no' a hen. You'll do better to…" Lilias stopped as she felt the slide of cold heat on her flesh. "Kiaran, mount your horse." She swung up into the saddle. "Quickly. We're no' alone."

He frowned and looked past her, searching the forest. "I see naught. Mayhap 'tis Broden, checking his traps."

She spun around until she saw the glint of silvered eyes glaring down at her from the trees. The Sluath watching them stretched out his black wings, which glittered with feathers like charred blades. Silver claws shoved aside a clump of leaves to reveal a beautiful face twisted with hatred, but the demon no longer gazed at her.

The Sluath looked at Kiaran with death glittering in his colorless eyes, and lifted a bow fitted with an iron-tipped arrow.

Someday ye shall ken what 'tis to sacrifice yerself for love, a soft voice said inside Lilias's mind. *I did. When the moment comes, ye go gladly, aye, eagerly.*

"No." She jerked on the mare's reins as she drove her heels into her sides. "You come for *me*."

Her horse knocked Kiaran aside as she bolted,

swerved away from the forest, and shot toward the stronghold.

Never shall I regret a moment I've had with ye, the lovely voice whispered. *Every torment I've suffered at the palace felt as a shadow of naught in the light of ye. Ye're my glory.*

Lilias clung to the reins and leaned low as she heard something slicing through the air. As the mare came to the outer edge of the maze, she jerked and abruptly stopped. With a scream of pain, the horse reared up, tossing Lilias from the saddle into the hedge.

Ye shall escape to the mortal realm, and find the Pritani, and live freely. Vow to me ye shall go.

Thorn-covered branches tore at her like hundreds of piercing whips as she fell heavily through the living wall. She landed with such force it drove the air from her lungs. Her ribs snapped like so many twigs. Pain became the world. Blood dripped from her mouth as she tried to lift her head, and then saw the vines uncoiling and dropping all around her. As they encircled her throat, Lilias dragged in one last breath.

She had lived a few days as a Pritani. Now she prayed that she would die as one.

As he pushed himself up from the ground, Kiaran felt an arrow slice through the air over his head. He saw Lilias clinging to the mare as she raced away from him, as if intending to draw fire. He glanced back at the trees as he drew his sword, but all he saw were some broken branches on the ground. The moment he took a step in that direction the mare screamed, and he heard the sound of hundreds of branches snapping, as if something had fallen through them. The commotion came from the maze, as if something had–

"Lilias."

He ran for the deadly labyrinth, but by the time he reached the outer hedge the horse had already bolted. The trap's dense growth had begun to fill in and close over a ragged gap. Through it he could see Lilias on the ground beyond, her garments wet with blood, her limbs entangled in vines and brambles.

His blood turned to ice as he saw the thick thorny vine tightening around her throat.

Swinging his blade, Kiaran hacked through the outer hedge, shearing off huge swaths of juniper to widen the gap again. The hedge lashed at his arms and chest, whipping him with dozens of thorny canes. Movement at his feet shifted his gaze to the vines creeping out from beneath the hedge toward his boots. He sliced through them with two vicious swipes of his sword before he pushed through the gap. Blood ran down his arms as he cut the vines away from Lilias's limbs to free her, and then wrenched her out of the writhing nest of bespelled brambles.

Blood trickled from her pale lips, and the vine that had cut deep into her neck still tightened over it.

With a roar of fury Kiaran ripped the green noose from her throat, revealing the terrible wound it had inflicted. She no longer breathed, and the limp sag of her body against him made him curse as he clamped his arm around her.

"You shallnae die on me, lass." He turned to chop at the rapidly-vanishing gap.

More branches smashed against Kiaran's back and shoulders, until at last he gathered all his strength and hurled himself through the hedge. On the other side he twisted, wrenching away from the twisting vines until he'd broken free of them.

He held onto his sword as he ran for the

closest cover, his tower retreat. Once inside he lowered Lilias onto his pallet and knelt down beside her. She did not move or breathe, and the ugly wound on her neck had stopped bleeding.

"I'll cut that facking maze into strew, my lady," he said softly as he brushed her hair back from her pale face. "Just as soon as you come back to me."

The sunlight faded, and all around Kiaran the tower grew dark. When he looked up, he saw the old stones growing together in rough-hewn stretches that curved over his head. When he looked at Lilias again his bed had vanished.

He now stood back in the secret chamber with her the night they had met, and held her against the wall. The vision they had shared after kissing had ended at this moment, and he tried to release her. His hands remained clamped on her arms, and outrage pulsed inside him with such force that he thought he might snap her bones.

"I dinnae believe ye," he heard himself say. "We're Pritani hunters. Mortals, just as ye. Our people dinnae become demons."

"Only the damned may change." Her throat moved as she swallowed. "'Tis the only reason you could pass through the gate, for it kills any ordinary mortal who crosses its threshold. The five of you now become Sluath, or die in transformation."

"I'm no' one of those facking things," Kiaran shouted.

"No' yet, Warrior." Her gaze searched his face. "Yet even now I can feel the hatred and rage inside you, and 'tis growing. 'Tis what brought you and your brothers beyond the brink of damnation, and permitted you enter the underworld."

Kiaran removed his hands and turned his back on her, his shoulders hunching. "'Tisnae truth. How could ye ken such? You're but a slave."

"Aye," Lilias said, coming around him. "'Twas my choice. 'Tis how I hide the truth of myself from Prince Iolar, and all his demons. 'Tis how I yet live, for if they learned who sired me, I'd be torn apart."

He scowled at her. "What matters yer sire to such creatures?"

"I shall tell you," she said, taking his hands in hers, "if you reveal your secret. What did you before coming through the gate that 'twould damn your soul?"

From his memory came the night when he'd

looked into dark blue eyes, so like his own, and watched them fill with tears. *Taye.* Her beloved face shifted into the hard, stern visage of Nectan, the Mag Raith headman, and the chilly contempt in his eyes.

Speak the truth and ye'll die. Hold yer tongue and ye'll live.

Kiaran pushed Lilias away from him, only to collide with a wall of mossy ashlar. Light flared all around him as the strange hidden chamber shifted back into his tower retreat. Through the glow he saw Lilias on his pallet, still as death.

Something gripped him from within. He felt his back burning as he staggered from the wall, but before he could reach the bed the pain drove him to his knees. He doubled over, writhing as he felt his brace and tunic tearing apart. The flesh beneath them did the same.

"End me, then," Kiaran groaned as he pressed his face against the cold stone floor.

Forces from within wrenched at his flesh until he thought his body would be torn in half. Then colder, damp air came in, fluttering through the faded tartan curtain to bathe him in the smell of rain.

His hands shook as he reached up and tore

the remains of his tunic and brace from his bloodied torso. The pain faded as he rocked back on his heels and slowly stood. The new weight on his shoulders nearly sent him toppling backward. He slapped a hand against the wall to hold himself upright, and looked down to see his flesh glowing a fiery golden-red color, as if he burned from within like a hearth. He turned his head to see what now cast twin long, curved shadows over Lilias.

Wings, fully grown and covered in fiery feathers, now arched from his back.

Chapter Fifteen

GALAN KNEW THE commotion caused by his attack would bring out the entire clan. Quickly he hurried away from the stronghold, cursing himself as he ran for his lack of control. Seeing Fiana in the flesh was impossible, and yet there she had been. His beloved, his reason for enduring, his deceitful, faithless bitch of a wife. Somehow she had cheated death, and come to Dun Chaill to join the clan. As they all shared Pritani blood she likely looked upon the Mag Raith as her kin. Or had she somehow enlisted their aid in the distant past?

White-hot rage swelled inside Galan as it all came clear to him. Somehow Domnall and the hunters must have helped Fiana feign her death in order to escape him. *That* was why she'd been smiling when Galan had watched her pretend to die. She'd been reveling over how easily she'd duped her mate with the ruse, leaving him to deal with the son she'd pretended to want so much.

Leaving me so she could play hoor for her five new lovers.

Of course, that explained the rest of it. Fiana would have been with the Mag Raith when they'd entered the underworld. He'd seen the proof of that in the Sluath skinwork on her right hand. Like them she had been made immortal by the demons. Indeed, with her beauty, wiles, and will she would have thrived in the underworld. Hadn't she tricked her mate to devote centuries to finding the means to bring her back to life? How she must have gloated over his idiocy. Her cruelty would have made the demons cherish her.

Until she betrayed them as well.

A bitter chuckle erupted from Galan, and he almost wished he hadn't burned the Sluath to ash. All this time Prince Iolar had been convinced that one of his own had turned against him, freed the Mag Raith and their wenches, and sealed off the underworld.

Fiana had been the traitor.

He retrieved the dead spy's remains and cloaked himself with the corpse to cross the barrier. By the time he found his horse most of his fury had settled. To capture Fiana he would need to bespell some mortals to take her from the stronghold while he dealt with the clan. Since the Sluath had emptied all the surrounding farms and villages of their occupants that meant traveling to the midlands, something he could do faster by flying once the storm arrived.

I'll take her to the old settlement. He imagined marching her to the edge of the grave he'd emptied—her grave, from which he'd stolen some other female's bones. He would force her to confess to all her trickery. Then he would fly off with her to some remote spot where he could punish her at his leisure. How she would plead for his love as he inflicted on her all the suffering he had endured.

Galan's cock hardened as he imagined feeding on her agony as he tormented her. Since she had attained immortality, she'd never die. He could see to it that she suffered for all eternity.

Mounting his horse, Galan took up the reins and looked toward the north. The smudge of dirty smoke above the ridges made him wish he hadn't burned all the Sluath to ash. To save their miserable hides, some of the demons might have sworn loyalty to him. Even now they could be attacking Dun Chaill. As for mortals, none could ever fight as fiercely as the Sluath, except…

The Skaraven.

As he rode away from the barrier, Galan felt as if all his lifetimes had come together in this moment. In his first incarnation he and Fiana had been ordered by the druid council to breed a son who would be an indentured warrior and their Skaraven spy. His odious son, Ruadri, had been the result. Galan had been forced to train the lad, whom he despised, as a shaman and a spy. He'd never allowed his son to forget that, by being born, he'd murdered his mother.

His mouth took on a bitter curl. *Mayhap I should beg the lad's forgiveness.*

Galan had rejoiced to hear Ruadri had died with the rest of the Skaraven fighting against a pair of rogue druids and their army of giants. Twelve centuries later Bhaltair Flen had awakened the entire clan of indentured warriors and granted them eternal life so they might protect the druids against their old enemy, also made immortal.

Clever and powerful as the rogues and their giants had been, nothing could stop the Skaraven.

To learn that Fiana not only lived but had been made immortal would bring the lad and his clan running to rescue her, especially if Galan convinced them that evil immortals held her prisoner. All he need do was cloak himself with an illusion that made him appear to be that meddling old fool Flen. Then, while the Skaraven and Mag Raith battled, he'd take Fiana.

The smell of something burnt dragged Galan from his plotting, and he glanced around in time to see a well of shadow stretching around him and his mount. Then the crushing weight of a huge body fell atop him, knocking him out of the saddle and pinning him to the ground.

"Hello, Aedth." White teeth flashed in Danar's half-blackened face as he drove one of his blades through Galan's palm. "Keeping busy, I see. Do you know, you've got dead human all over you? You really should have taken time to bathe after crawling out of the pit."

"No. 'Tisnae possible." The pain of being skewered barely registered, so great was his shock at seeing the big demon. "I set fire to the village so that you'd burn. All of you."

"Many of our brethren died in the flames, but not all." Danar pushed himself upright so that he straddled him, and pulled on thick gloves before he removed a large, toothed torque from his belt.

Before Galan realized what he meant to do he clamped and locked it around his neck. "No." Immediately he felt the iron burn into his neck. "Release me, or I shall–"

"Kill me? Even after having your throat cut, you're still a dreamer." The Sluath shook his head as he attached a silver chain to the torque's ringed hasp and lumbered to his feet. "Your new neckpiece is a punishment collar I took the last time I culled a slaver ship. The more you resist, the deeper the teeth sink. You've seen what damage iron does to our bodies. If I jerk it hard enough, it will shear off your head."

Galan stopped struggling. "Why no' do that now and end me?"

"I already have once today, and I hate to repeat myself." Danar grinned as he jerked on the chain, causing the collar's spikes to bite deeper into his flesh. "Besides, our prince is waiting for you in the ridges. You didn't kill him, either."

Chapter Sixteen

❦

AN ALL-TOO-familiar sensation roused Lilias from what she had thought her death. Light danced against her skin, brighter even than the sunshine of Kiaran's world, yet leeched of all its gentle warmth. As she shrank from the ugly glare, tangled memories began to unsnarl in her mind. Once more she saw herself taking Kiaran through the tunnels, hiding him in her secret chamber, revealing that terrible truth to him. All of that she had done, and more. Yet the remembrance had ended before the moment that had forever changed her.

Now the icy air biting into her flesh told her that she lay in the presence of a demon.

Had the vines choking her somehow dragged her body beneath the castle, into the tunnels, and pushed her through the old gate? When she opened her eyes would she find herself trapped again in the underworld, again to be made a slave? Why had she been denied a merciful end? Hadn't she earned that much?

A deep, wrenching groan brought Lilias fully awake.

When she propped herself up she saw the cuts on her hands and arms closing and shrinking. Across from her Kiaran stood braced against the tower wall, his head bowed, his body glowing. The light had spread out from the skinwork on his arm, which rippled with white and blue shimmers that reflected off the scrolls of frost forming on the stone wall around his flattened hands.

The alterations to his appearance stunned her, for his red-gold hair now gleamed as if spun from a sunset, while his darkly-tanned flesh appeared to be paling. Dozens of wounds on his arms and chest had begun to close like her own, but what arched up from his spine made her go still.

He'd already grown the wings of a Sluath.

"Kiaran." Lilias dragged herself from the bed,

ignoring the weakness of her still-healing body to go to him. "You must fight the change."

He tried to push her away. "'Tis too late."

"Only if you yield." She moved closer, pressing herself against him as she lifted her inked hand to his face. Her magic lit up her skinwork and raced across his shoulder to flood into his. "In the underworld you vowed to me you wouldnae surrender to it. Remember now. Remember me."

K*IARAN'S* *EYES* filled with shimmering light. Through it he could see Lilias's beauty changing, just as the despair and self-hatred inside him faded like old wraiths. In his thoughts he felt her now as never before, her gentleness permeating every corner of his mind. She moved through him like a cool, sweet breeze, and more came in her wake. He could feel the terrible blankness of the past beginning to crumble, and then he saw her there, too.

My lovely lass.

Aye, m'anam, *my soul. I've found you again, as I vowed I would.*

His body shook as he held her tightly, and she drew his head down to touch her brow to his. The stream of time that had separated them for so long now receded like his dark emotions. Again, he found himself in the vision of that night when he and his brothers had entered the tunnels beneath the fortress. Now he saw past the frantic moments of their escape, past his retreat into her chamber, to what they had become to each other as she kept him from finishing the terrible change.

I dinnae wish to become a demon, Kiaran told her, sounding utterly defeated as he pressed a dagger into her hands. *Ye must end me before I change.*

'Tis but three things that halt the change, Warrior. Lilias pulled off her ragged garments, and stood before him clad only in blue-white light. *Love freely given, 'tis one.*

Kiaran felt pity and desire battle inside him as he looked upon her, for surely she was the loveliest female he'd ever beheld. He'd never wanted any lass more. Yet she had been born a slave, and doubtless cruelly used. He would not take advantage of her to serve his selfish lusts.

Ye neednae offer me yer body, lass. I'm no' a demon to ravage ye, even with my worthless heart.

'Tisnae worthless to me, Kiaran mag Raith, and I've never lain with mortals or demons. Lilias gazed at him with all the hope of a maiden, but none of the fear. *I've waited to ken pleasure all my life. Willnae you teach me?*

Hearing that she had never been touched made him feel even more wretched, but it was the soft touch of her hand on his arm that smashed through his resolve. Kiaran took hold of her fingers and brought them to his lips before he drew her over to the silk-strewn divan.

Lilias reached for the bottom of his tunic and drew it up over his head.

※

As THE MEMORY of their first night together faded away, so did the glow from Kiaran's flesh. Lilias saw his wings fold behind his back before vanishing, and felt his body warming against hers. Even if she had risked their lives by doing so, she had not been too late to save him.

"You truly gave yourself to me, that night I found you in the tunnels?" he murmured.

"Aye." She traced the hard line of his jaw with

her fingertips. "As did I every night after, to keep you from changing."

"You've never forgotten me, or that facking place." Kiaran wrapped his arms around her, lifting her off her feet as he brought her up to his eye level. He looked more confused than angry, which also reassured her. "Why didnae you say?"

"You swore me to silence before we parted," she admitted. "You made me vow to tell you naught when I again found you. You feared… without me the change would be complete, and I'd find you made Sluath."

"Nearly you did. You should have used my dagger that night." He placed her back on her feet, and moved away from her. "'Tis yet time to correct your choice."

Lilias didn't understand what he meant until she saw him reach for his sword.

"As you wish." Her fingers trembled as she pulled the dagger from his hip sheath, for she knew what it would do to her. Yet living without him would be worse that dying.

Kiaran drew the blade. "You'll be safe with the clan."

"You willnae leave me behind again." As he turned she touched the tip to a space just below her left breast, and nodded to him. "I go with you."

He swore and snatched the blade from her, tossing it away before he pulled her against him. "You cannae save me, lass. No' in the underworld, and no' here."

"You're mistaken." She wound her arms around his neck. "We shall save each other."

"How?" Kiaran demanded.

"As we did the night we met." Lilias tugged loose the bodice laces of her gown, and let it slip from her shoulders. "We've this time alone together." She worked the garment down to her waist and let it fall to the floor. The sunlight coming through the old tartan made her bare body glow. "I'd be yours again."

His eyes darkened as he looked down at her jutting breasts before he turned away. "I've naught to offer you but a hard cock, lass. You need more than that."

"I need to be close to you. To feel you as part of me." Lilias reached for the laces of his trews, untying them before boldly slipping her hands inside and around his lean hips. His long, heavy shaft brushed against her fingertips, so hard it felt like silk-wrapped stone. She pressed her brow against the back of his shoulder. "Please, Kiaran. I've thought of naught else since you kissed me."

His body went rigid against hers, and then he spun and seized her. Before she could blink she lay beneath him on his bed, the frame shuddering around them from the force of their landing.

He shoved down his trews, and took hold of her thighs, parting them as he guided his straining cockhead to her wet quim. The moment his sex touched hers she arched up, inviting him inside her body, desperate to feel him there.

For all his rough urgency Kiaran didn't ram his shaft into her softness. Instead he watched her face as he inched between her clenching folds, as careful and restrained as he'd been with her that first joining. His cock seemed to caress the slick, tender flesh within as he gave her more and more, filling her until she moaned with the sweet ache of his claiming.

When he had skewered her to his root, he bent his head and brushed his mouth over her open lips, her eyelids and the curve of her ear. There he murmured, "Gods, but you're as a night bloom filled with dew."

"I'm not a flower," Lilias assured him, and slipped her hands around him to cup his tight buttocks. "I'm your lass, as ever I've been. Touch me. Kiss me. Fack me."

Her begging made his eyes burn with hot lust, and then he did all that she asked. His mouth ravaged hers, his tongue taking hers as he filled his hands with her breasts. Between her thighs he began moving, thrusting deeper before drawing out, his shaft working inside her with hard, heavy deliberation.

"Now you wish to make me yours," Kiaran said, his voice rumbling from the depths of his chest. "That I might fack you each night again, my pretty lady. In another life never should you wander sleepless for want of my cock."

"'Twas why I came from the stronghold that night," she whispered. "I'd hoped to climb in your bed and lay with you while you slept."

"Brazen wench." He squeezed her mound. "Tell me the rest of your scheme. Did you reckon you'd wake me, seduce me?"

She shook her head. "I wished to pleasure myself as I breathed you in, and looked upon you."

Kiaran took hold of her wrist, and drew her hand down between them, and then shifted back so he could see her quim. "Show me."

Lilias bit her bottom lip as she parted her quim, and rubbed a fingertip over the throbbing nub. When she would have taken her hand back Kiaran shook his head.

"Dinnae stop." He began to move again, penetrating her in time with the gentle strokes she gave her pearl. "Aye, just so."

Lilias's hand shook as she lost herself in his loving and her own. To know he watched her pleasuring herself as he did the same made her feel so wanton she whimpered. Soon her hips began to move on their own, thrusting up against her hand as he impaled her over and over, immersing her in a flood of heat and sensation. As he plucked at her tight nipples he thrust harder and faster, and then took her lips in another demanding kiss.

The hungry need of his mouth made her head spin, but his ravishing hands and rampant cock and her own stroking set the world around them to tilt, and then explode. Lilias heard her own cries as the pleasure took her, and felt him shudder and groan as he followed, and then collapsed and rolled away from her.

Nothing in her life had ever felt so good, or so

right. All she would ever need was this man, and his love.

Lilias turned to curl against him, her body still quaking with echoes of that startling, stunning release. He'd compelled her to do as they'd never done in the underworld, and now she wondered how much more there was for them to discover. Her lips curved as she imagined all the nights he'd spend teaching her again.

Kiaran turned and propped himself up on his elbow as he regarded her, but the passion no longer burned in his eyes. "Tell me. Did I get you with child in the underworld? Did you leave my bairn there?"

The question didn't startle her as much as the coldness of his voice. "I'm barren. 'Twas why my *máthair* hid me from my sire. She reckoned he'd end me when he found he couldnae breed me like her."

"'Tis good." He climbed off the bed. "I wouldnae wish to leave you with an unwanted bairn. Mayhap your other lovers felt the same."

"'Twouldnae be thus, and no other has taken me." She sat up, frowning as she watched him dress. "I wish I'd bear you a son or daughter. I think we'd make a beautiful bairn."

"'Tisnae all that matters, even beauty as heart-rending as yours." He brought her gown and pulled it over her head before he tugged her to her feet. "Come with me."

She followed him up the stairs into the aviary, which appeared to be finished. Everywhere she looked, however, she now saw newly-placed iron bars. He'd fixed them over the window slits, the walls, floor and ceiling. "You mean to trap your birds?"

"No' the raptors." He gave her a gentle push toward the center of the floor, and then retreated down the steps. As soon as he did a wall of iron bars dropped down between them, blocking the stairs. "I built this trap for you before I came to take you on patrol."

She stared at him through the iron she dared not touch. "You'd cage me here? Why?"

"I ken that you're Prince Iolar's treasure." Kiaran spat the accusation like a curse. "Lady Nellie touch-read the shell pendant you wore. She saw how the demons kept you, like something precious. You lied to me. What slave wears silk gowns and jewels?"

"'Tisnae what you reckon," Lilias said quickly.

"I didnae tell you of the prince, but nor would I lie to you."

He made a terse gesture. "Then reveal what you ken of the underworld. Tell me the name of the traitor who freed us, and why he sent us to Dun Chaill. Give me every truth you've hidden, and I shall release you."

Lilias took a step back. Although he now knew they had become lovers in the underworld, most of his memories of her remained locked in darkness. In order for their plan to work they would have to stay shrouded until the Sluath came.

"I cannae tell you more." In that moment she hated herself more than he did. "Only trust that soon I shall."

"Had I the time to wait." A strange look came over his face. "Farewell, my lady."

She rushed to the bars, pushing her hand through the iron in a desperate attempt to touch him, but he'd already retreated down the stairs. The cold metal burned into her flesh as she yanked back her hand, and stared at the wisps of smoke rising from the black marks left on her knuckles and fingers. The bars on the floor did the same to her bare feet as she staggered backward.

Lilias felt the first surge of weakness as she

tore the sleeves from her gown, and used them to wrap her burned feet. As she wrapped her arms around her waist, she looked again at all the lethal iron around her.

If Kiaran did not soon return, his beautiful aviary would become her tomb.

Chapter Seventeen

DELICIOUS SCENTS FROM the great hall greeted Kiaran as he walked through the kitchens. Seeing the clan sat gathered around the table finishing their midday meal made him wonder if he'd chosen the right course. All of the other hunters had their mates beside them, and always would. Thanks to the Sluath they would have each other forever.

Thanks to his own treachery, he'd never have the same with Lilias.

"Fair day, Brother," Broden greeted him, a knowing gleam in his dark eyes. "I came to summon you and your lady to dine with us, but your wee screechers chased me off."

"I've set aside some pastries for you both," Rosealise said, rising from the bench.

"If you'd stay, my lady." Although resolved, Kiaran felt the terrible temptation to turn and walk out. He could take his half-demon lover and leave Dun Chaill, and the clan would never know why. But in what was left of his heart he knew he could no longer keep from them the truth. "I've barricaded Lilias in my tower aviary. She survived falling into the maze, and healed from wounds that would kill a mortal. She hasnae lost her memories. Once I'm finished, you should question her."

"Finished what?" Domnall asked.

"I've also concealed much from the clan," he told him as he pulled off his tunic.

Summoning his wings took only a moment. They appeared and spread out on either side of him. The firelight made them look as if they burned with red and gold light as he lowered them to his sides. No one at the table moved or blinked, but at least none of the hunters reached for their blades.

"They began to sprout again just after my back wounds healed," Kiaran told Domnall before he regarded Edane. "I hid them under a brace strapped to my back and told you 'twas bandaging."

The chieftain rose to his feet, and walked around the table to stand between the clan and Kiaran. "'Tis the true reason you've been so distant."

He nodded. "I kept silent, and waited to see what more of me would alter. 'Twas my plan to sink a blade in my heart before I became wholly demon. Then, when Lilias came, the coldness left me, and I began to feel again. I've no desire to harm the clan."

"I never reckoned you would," Domnall said. "Your body may change, but at heart you're Mag Raith."

"You're wrong." He regarded the other hunters. "From the beginning I lied to you, all of you. I never lived among the Pritani before your tribe took me in."

"What say you?" Broden frowned. "Your people cast you out?"

"No." Kiaran folded his wings, and wished them away. "They sailed to this land to raid your settlements. Those they couldnae enslave they killed. On their final journey, I came with them."

TELLING the clan his story took Kiaran back to that terrible voyage, and all he had tried to forget since arriving in Caledonia.

As a boy he had crouched deep in the hold of the leaking longboat, his boots and trews soaked by the bilge water. The journey had taken so long that they had eaten what little food they'd brought, and his empty belly hurt. Soon he would be too weak to stay awake. Still the oars above them creaked back and forth, and the icy sea pounded against the hull, ready to swallow them.

Just as Kiaran thought he might weep with despair, a shout of a sighting came from the upper deck. The sound of the waves went from crashing to lapping.

At long last they had reached land.

"Say naught of what I told ye," Taye whispered in her tongue, the language they spoke to each other only when no one else could hear. "Should they find ye, tell them ye came to fight with Thane Njal. No matter what comes to pass, never go back to Noreg with them. 'Tis yer land and people here."

Njal, the towering brute who owned Taye,

terrified Kiaran. He would run away from the boatyards whenever he saw the gleam of his long white-gold hair.

He clutched his mother's arm. "Dinnae leave me," he begged. His fingers dug into her intricate skinwork, his nails making it seem as though the inked bird there bled.

Gently, she took his hand away. "Be a good, brave lad for me now." She wrapped him in the one damp blanket they had shared on the voyage, tucking it around his thin, shivering limbs. "I love ye, my son."

Her lips trembled as she kissed his brow, and then she slipped away from the casks. She climbed up the side of the hull, opened the narrow cargo hatch, and crawled through.

For a moment he felt a wail of despair rising in his throat, but swallowed it. She would go and find her tribe, and come back for him. She had sworn on Odin's beard that she would. Then his *máthair's* people would kill the raiders and free Kiaran and Taye. They would never have to go back to the *jarl's* settlement. They would live in Caledonia as Pritani, and Njal would never beat Taye again.

Kiaran curled up, blinking back his tears as he

listened to the sounds above him. He knew the *jarl* had sent Njal and his raiders to take people from other lands as slaves. The strongest would be sold at the slave market for much gold. The rest would be housed with the stock and forced to work long and hard in the boatyards with little rest and bad food. The Norsemen also often used the females for pleasure, as Njal did Taye.

This time they shallnae enslave my people, Kiaran thought as he dozed off. *Taye will bring the Pritani to kill them all.*

"We've water enough for the return," a loud voice said in the darkness, waking Kiaran. "These here remain untapped. But this shall be the last voyage of this olden bitch. The bilge fair overflows."

Kiaran went still as the cask hiding him shifted.

"By Thor's scorched teeth." The angry giant yanked Kiaran from where he cowered, lifting him off his feet to dangle above the deck like hook bait. "How got ye here, tadpole?"

Hanging there should have made Kiaran writhe with terror, but being called small made him furious.

"Let go of me, *istrumagi*." A fist clouted the

side of his head, and the wail he'd fought to hold burst from his lips. "Harm me, and my people shall take much time slaying ye."

The giant flung back his head and laughed. "We're yer people, ye simpleton." He turned his head toward the front of the longboat. "Thane Njal, come down here. I've found yer *oskilgetinn* hiding his skinny arse by our water."

Njal swung down into the hold, peering through the darkness at Kiaran. "Gods plague me, 'tis Taye's get. I left the puny bastart picking rivets with the keel master. How comes my bastart on the raid?"

Kiaran stared back at the Viking raider. "Ye're no' my sire. I'm Pritani, just as my *máthair*."

Laughing now, Njal strode up and seized him, dragging him close to his face.

"Ye need learning, lad," the thane told him. "I facked Taye until her belly swelled with ye. No other touched her. I saw to that. Then when she whelped ye, 'twas my blade cut the cord."

"I'm Pritani," Kiaran insisted.

The thane studied his face for a long moment. "Taye wouldnae let her beloved whelp out of her sight. She'd cut her own throat first." Njal dropped him and began pulling aside the casks. "Where hides that pretty whore?"

"Ye'll no' find her," Kiaran shouted, and then clamped a hand over his mouth, but it was too late. For all that he'd promised his mother, he'd just betrayed her.

Njal dragged him to the upper deck, where he shoved him against the main mast and tied him there. "Bring me my whip."

"*No, please.*" Kiaran had watched the thane whip slaves. He'd seen the horror those beatings had left on their backs. Some had even died of the wounds. "She ran away, through the cargo hatch."

※

"I DIDNAE ken what would come from what I'd revealed to Njal," Kiaran admitted to the clan. "Had I held my tongue, or claimed myself alone, my sire wouldnae have found her."

"But you were just a frightened boy," Jenna said, her sympathy plain.

"You're kind, my lady." More so than he deserved, Kiaran thought. "Yet my words enraged my sire, and decided my *máthair's* fate. Njal took me with him and his raiders as they hunted Taye. Her tracks led them to her tribe's settlement."

He told them how the Vikings had surrounding the Pritani village, and launched a surprise attack with fire and weapons.

"In the confusion I broke free from my sire," Kiaran said. "The screams of the dying followed me as I ran away from the settlement."

Edane sighed. "And from that horror you came to our tribe."

"No' that night," he admitted. "I hid in the forest, and near dawn I crept back to see if my *máthair* yet lived."

※

THIN LIGHT SHONE through the haze of smoke by the time Kiaran crawled into the brush surrounding the settlement. He held his breath when he saw Njal dragging Taye by the hair out of the smoldering ruins of the village. As the thane flung her before the other raiders and drew his sword, Kiaran bit down on his tongue to keep from screaming for her.

"Ye should never have tried to escape with the lad," the Viking told her. "Had ye served me well,

I might have freed ye both someday. Now call and bid him come to ye. He's somewhere in the trees."

Kiaran tasted blood as he crouched down. His mother turned her head and for a moment he thought she saw him, for a small smile curved her lips. Then she looked up at Njal, and a terrible calm came over her battered face.

"Ye shall free me now, ye evil bastart," Taye told the Viking. "Then ye shall ken my vengeance. Never again shall ye see my son."

"As ye desire, ye foolish whore." Njal raised his blade, and brought it down through her neck.

Nausea swept through Kiaran, and he couldn't help but moan. But the cheers of the other raiders kept him from being heard. He stared as the men scattered, taking what little they could find among the blackened remains of the settlement. The last to leave was Njal, who looked out at the surrounding forest for a long moment.

"Come with me, lad," he called, "and I shall free ye. Indeed, I shall name ye my son before the *jarl*. Ye have my word, ye shall be raised up as what ye're born: a Viking."

For a moment Kiaran felt the weight of that promise. What remained of his mother's tribe would not survive the night. He knew nothing of this land except the language Taye had taught him. He also knew how much Njal and his kind were despised. If he ever told the Pritani that he had been sired by a Viking slaver, they would likely cut his throat.

Never go back with them, Taye had said.

He had caused her death. If nothing else he would honor his mother's wish. Nothing more came to him as a great blackness swallowed him whole.

In the night Kiaran awoke to the sounds of owls calling and the wind whispering through the trees surrounding the flower-filled meadow where he lay. He burrowed deeper into the fragrant lilies and closed his eyes, knowing that if a predator came upon him he might never again wake. Yet at first light he sat up, cold and tired but unharmed.

The Gods had not finished with him.

Days and nights passed uncounted as Kiaran kept walking and falling and sleeping and rising. He ate berries and nuts and sometimes handfuls of heather, just to fill the hollow in his belly. His garments shredded as he waded through brush and brambles and thickets. He grew filthy, his hair tangling into a snarl of burs and grass and knots. His feet cracked and bled and blackened.

Yet every morning he woke to begin walking again.

He had no sense of direction, only to go as far from the place of his mother's murder as he could. The sound of women laughing drew him out of the forest to a place filled with fruit trees. There he saw dozens of females dressed in long tunics and skirts gathering baskets of gold and green pears. They all wore their hair as Taye had, in lovely braided coils looped around their heads. Some had skinwork with intricate designs of animals and symbols etched along their arms and throats and cheeks.

One of the older women saw him and let out a cry.

Suddenly baskets dropped and pears bounced and rolled into the grass as all of the females came running toward him. He stared at them, waiting for them to see what he was and attack, but when they reached for him their hands felt warm and gentle, and their eyes filled with kindness and sorrow.

"Where come ye from, lad?" the older woman asked.

Kiaran's throat felt too dry and tight to allow him to speak. He turned and pointed to the smudge of smoke on the horizon. He came from Taye, from her tribe, from the Pritani.

"By the Gods." The older woman picked him up in her arms and hurried with him through the pear trees. "Call Nectan. We've found a lost bairn."

Kiaran looked at the sprawling village that lay beyond the orchard, and saw other boys like him rushing out of round-topped longhouses to stare back at him. One thin, pale lad had bright red hair. Beside him a much larger boy with gentle eyes rested a giant hand on his shoulder. They were joined by a beautiful dark lad with a sullen face, and a tall, stern-featured boy who had green eyes like Taye.

I shall never tell them, he thought, and then blinked against the sting of tears.

Chapter Eighteen

✦

FROM WITHIN THE shelter of the cave Prince Iolar felt madness and power sift through the air. He dropped the limp body of the shepherdess his demons had brought to him and strode out to see Danar leading a horse up the slopes. Behind the mount followed a greatly changed Galan Aedth. The big demon held a chain connected to an iron collar around the transformed druid's blackened throat. The stench of burning Sluath flesh grew thick.

"It seems Danar has brought another gift for you, my prince." Clamhan lifted his skull mask, but as soon as he tasted the air he dropped it down and scuttled back. "Do you feel that? He's been transformed *and* tormented beyond reason."

"One should not skimp when bestowing favors, I find." Iolar walked down to the big demon, who bowed and presented him with the chain. "Excellent work for a change. I especially like how you've gift-wrapped him for me. When I take the time to slaughter the useless, you will not be among them."

"I shall attempt to show proper gratitude for your generosity later, my prince." Danar eyed Galan. "But I'd keep the collar on him. He's off in his own realm, and it's not a happy place."

"You." The druid's lips peeled back from his gleaming teeth to form a ferocious sneer in his beautiful face. "You did this to me."

"Still as dim as ever, I see. That's rather disappointing." Iolar tugged down on the chain until Galan dropped to his knees. "There, now you're in the proper position to pay homage to your new liege. You should thank me for ridding you of the last shreds of your humanity. Which you may do now." He waited, and then rolled his free hand. "Any time now, Aedth."

"Fack you," the druid spat the words.

Even muted by the iron collar, the malevolent forces radiating from Galan enveloped Iolar like a huge, icy fist. He'd never known a mortal to change into a demon who possessed so much power upon awakening to immortality. The magic he had given the druid before his change must have played a part. In his weakened condition Iolar knew he would never be able to defeat Galan as a *deamhan*, so taking his head now seemed the most prudent course. Yet with some careful handling he might be able to control the druid, and make use of all that lovely power he'd attained.

For the prince, the promise of might always eclipsed fear-spawned caution. The only time he'd managed both was when he'd murdered the king.

Iolar crouched down. "I gave you exactly what you wanted, Fledgling: immortality and the strength to thwart and crush your enemies." He saw a flicker of new hatred flare in the druid's black eyes. "You went after the Mag Raith by yourself, didn't you? What happened?"

"Fiana found her way to Dun Chaill. I saw her with Kiaran mag Raith. You always ken that she yet lived. You made her immortal. I saw the skinwork." Galan's claws curled around the slave collar. "Take this facking torque from me."

His babbling perplexed Iolar, who stood and

walked over to Danar. "Did *you* cull the wife, and not tell me of her?"

"No, my prince. The druid has always been something of a lunatic about that dead female," the big demon reminded him. "Only now he has enough power to finish what he started in the village."

Rain began to fall all around them, pattering gently on the weathered stone of the slopes.

"I shall tear off your head," Galan promised as he struggled with the collar, and wisps of smoke rose from his burning hands. "And your cock. And stuff both up that oversize grice's arse–"

"You'll be too busy," Iolar told him. "Even you must know that you've become the most powerful demon here. None of us may ever challenge you and survive." As Galan continued to spout threats, he told the other demons, "When we return to the underworld, I can no longer rule the Sluath."

"My prince," Clamhan said uneasily, slipping off his skull mask. "You may wish to rethink your abdication. Aedth is obviously deranged. We'd never survive his rule."

Merineal's childlike face twisted into a scowl.

"I for one don't wish to be commanded by a tree-licker. They stink of dried greenery and pointless ritual, and taste of dirt."

Seabhag shifted into an exact replica of the shepherdess, and draped himself with her blood-stained cloak. "If you no longer want the throne, my prince, I'll be happy to–"

"*Silence,*" Danar shouted. "The strongest rules the horde. That is how it has always been decided."

All of the demons gaped at him before wisely shutting their mouths.

Iolar suppressed a smirk as he helped Galan to his feet. "So, Aedth, it seems you've arrived at your destiny. I never would have guessed it." He scanned the dismayed faces of his *deamhanan*. "I wish you much luck with ruling the Sluath."

The druid left off his ranting and peered at him. "What did you say?"

"As soon as we return to the underworld, the throne is yours." Sounding humbled took some effort, but Iolar did his best as he sketched a shallow bow. "All that I ask in return is that you first help us defeat the rebels, and force their shaman to reopen the gates."

Galan's upper lip curled. "I will do naught for you. You had me killed."

"You had to die a mortal death in order to transform," Iolar patiently reminded him. "Danar should have mentioned that. But let us move past your necessary murder and delightful rebirth. What I propose is that we combine our power, and augment the storm. Once we can assure that it will last for days, not hours, we'll raid the rebels' hiding place with our brethren, and help you take your vengeance."

"Why should I trust you?" the druid demanded.

"You shouldn't—without proof that I trust you." Tasting Galan's greed reassured him, so he unlatched the slave collar, removed it, and tossed it away. "There. That is how much I trust you, my liege." For good measure he knelt down before the druid. "Let us assure that the Mag Raith become no more than a happy memory of pain and slaughter. Let me help you reclaim your Fiana, to do with as you please."

For a moment no one moved as Galan bowed his head and spread his silvered black wings. The air around him grew so dense with cold that the falling rain froze and plummeted to the ground in tear-shaped drops of white ice. Just as the prince wondered if he had assumed too much, the druid held out his claws.

"Thank you, Brother." As Iolar took hold of the new demon's hands and stood, he felt all that lovely power flooding into him. He channeled what he needed to his body, from which all the deterioration began to recede. "Together we will make the storm swallow the skies for as long as we wish."

Chapter Nineteen

※

KIARAN COULDN'T MAKE himself look into the eyes of the men he'd considered friends since their first hunt, and brothers since their last. Once he finished his account of what he had done, and his shameful origin as the son of a Viking raider and a Pritani slave, he felt dead inside. Speaking the truth had been more scalding than cleansing, as if the words had burned away what little feeling he had left.

"Why didnae you ever tell us?" Domnall finally asked.

"At first I feared what would befall me if I revealed the truth to the tribe," he admitted. "Yet for all the deaths I caused when I came here from Noreg, 'twas what I did for your murderous sire that caused our damnation. 'Twas my true betrayal of you and my brothers."

Domnall's eyes narrowed. "You ken he meant to end me?"

That the chieftain knew of the headman's plan stunned Kiaran. "When did you learn of his scheme?"

"Tell me first how you discovered what Nectan had planned," Domnall said.

"The day before we left the tribe for the last time, I saw your sire in the forest with a pair of Romans." He saw Broden stiffen. "I hid myself in the trees, and listened to them parlay. They planned to attack the settlement. Nectan offered five strong males if they would leave the Mag Raith in peace."

"'Twas a lie," Edane said, looking appalled. "Our tribe didnae keep slaves."

"Aye, but we ken the five he most despised." Broden's expression darkened. "'Twas us he pledged to the invaders as slaves."

"Worse than that," Kiaran said. "The Romans told Nectan they wished to use the five slaves as animals. They would be killed as blood sacrifices to their battle god, to insure their victory over all Pritani. Domnall's sire agreed."

Rosealise covered her gasp with her hand, and Mael closed his eyes and groaned. Now as pale as her mate, Nellie twined her fingers with Edane's. Mariena placed her arm around Broden's shoulder as he began to rise.

"Let him finish, *mon couer*," the Frenchwoman said.

"You called yourself my brother," Domnall said, his voice growing dangerously soft, "and never you uttered a word of this scheme to me."

Kiaran nodded. "Your sire discovered me watching him. He vowed he'd end me if I told you, and still you'd be sacrificed. If I kept silent, he'd give the Romans another in my place." He felt the old shame twist inside him like a dull blade stabbing deep. "No one would believe an outsider over the headman. I didnae wish to die for naught. When we left that day for the last hunt, I didnae intend to return."

"No, you wished to take the coward's path. You meant to run away again, leaving those who loved you to die," Broden said, his contempt as savage as his gaze. "And I reckoned you my brother in truth."

Kiaran considered telling them what he had done before they'd left on their final hunt, but he could never prove it.

"'Tis my fault, but all of you shared unknowingly in the wrong," he said, revealing the last of his terrible truths. "When we didnae return to the tribe, Nectan couldnae keep his bargain. Your kin never vanished, as Galan ever claimed. The Romans came and slaughtered them. 'Twas for the massacre of the Mag Raith I reckon that the Gods damned us all."

Domnall swore under his breath. "You cannae take blame for my sire's wrongs, or the evil he invited on our tribe."

"Someone must, and I'd settle the debt." Kiaran knelt down before the chieftain and offered him his sword. "I caused my sire to kill my *máthair* and her tribe. I never warned you of Nectan's scheme. I've betrayed my brothers with lies. I could become Sluath at any moment, and for my past wrongs I surely will. If in truth you ever regarded me as a brother, I beg you permit me die as a man, no' a demon."

All of the hunters rose and came to stand in a circle around him. At least none of them looked happy at the prospect of watching his beheading.

"Wait," Jenna said as she joined the men. "Kiaran, I can't begin to understand what you've been through, but what you said, I know that isn't the whole story." She took the sword from his hands, and looked at her mate. "You're not the only one with a secret."

"Indeed." Rosealise came and tucked her arm through Mael's. "After all this clan has suffered, I think it high time we sort out this damnation nonsense."

"Mais oui," Mariena put in as she walked over and took Broden's hand. "I killed so many Nazis I could not count, and I did not get the wings or the claws." She sniffed. "And look. Broden is still more beautiful than me."

"Well, if none of you want to chop off his head, I could do it." Nellie sauntered to Kiaran and eyed him for a long moment before she sighed and turned to Edane. "Only Jenny's right, lover boy. You need to make like the canary now."

The guilt on the other hunters' faces made Kiaran rise to his feet. "I dinnae understand."

"No matter what you did on the day of our last hunt, Nectan couldnae have kept his bargain with the Romans," Domnall said. "For I killed him the night before we left the settlement."

Chapter Twenty

✦

DESPITE HIS BODY wards, taking the pretty slave from the falconer's iron-barricaded tower had burned Culvar's hands and arms. More pain bloomed in his distorted leg and rammed up into his hip as he limped through his tunnels with her slung over his shoulder. Any amount of struggling on her part would have sent them both sprawling. Thankfully she had been unconscious, and so cold to the touch he at first thought her dead.

Something had wounded and drained the life from her.

"I never expected to see you again, little slave," he muttered to her as he slowly hobbled along, their combined weight making his walking stick creak in his damp grip. "I thought surely that my brother would have torn you apart after you freed me."

At last he arrived at his spell chamber, where two iron warriors stood guarding the entry. The moment they saw the slave girl both drew their blades, ready as ever to kill an intruder.

"Put down your weapons," Cul told them. "This one I want alive. Open the door."

Inside the chamber he took Lilias to the hunched, ice-clad figure standing in the spell circle, where he dropped her at the old man's feet. Torches flared to life around them, revealing the extent of her injuries. Dark welts on her hands and feet oozed blood, which aggravated him even more than the throbbing agony of his shattered leg.

"You must have amused the prince greatly to be revived so often," he chided the unconscious female, and then chuckled. "Good. We want Iolar to come for you, so don't die yet."

He tottered outside the circle, and then cast a barrier spell around his unwilling guests. Only then did he release the shaman from the frozen enchantment that gripped him.

For a long moment the wrinkled face of the

Pritani remained twisted in a snarl of contempt as he came back to life. Then Lilias moaned, and the shaman glanced down and knelt to look at her wounds.

"What did ye to her?" the old man demanded.

"I took her from an iron cage the intruders built in one of the towers," Cul told him. "It appears that before I arrived she harmed herself attempting to escape it."

The shaman took off his cloak and covered her with it as he peered at the deep welts on her hands. "Iron burns on her flesh. She's one of yer kind."

The rough, grating sound of Cul's laugh echoed around them. "I'm the only halfling born who survived my brother's murder of the king. She's one of their turned slaves, made immortal demon by whatever evil she did."

"She's no' a demon entire." The shaman peered up at him. "Ye didnae feel her heart? 'Tis beating like a mortal's, like yers."

Lilias's eyelids fluttered, and then she opened them. In the torchlight her eyes gleamed a gilded bronze, which they had never been in the underworld. As she focused on Cul she smiled as if his battered visage pleased her. She even reached out to him.

"Culvar," she said in the same, sweet, nameless voice that had haunted his dreams for centuries.

The shaman helped brace her as she struggled to her feet.

"Go carefully, lass. Ye've badly burned yer feet." He regarded Cul. "Take down the ward. She's too weak to do more than tumble on her face, ye great beast."

Banishing the spell barrier required only a flick of power. Cul did not cross into the circle, however, but summoned his iron warriors to flank him on either side, and more to stand ready out in the passage.

The old Pritani put his arm around Lilias and led her over to the nearest bench before he went to the potions cabinet. "I'll clean the burns before I dress them. She'll need some of yer power to heal."

"Away from the iron I'll recover now, Shaman." She extended her hands, which had stopped bleeding. "I've my own power."

Cul watched, fascinated now as the deep welts

paled and faded away. "You're as I am, and she was."

"Mayhap in the beginning. I cannae say. Much of me changed after you left the underworld." Lilias glanced around the chamber before meeting his gaze. "Our lady bid me find you when I arrived in the mortal realm. She wished me to ask if you kept your vow to her."

That she knew of his promise meant the beautiful slave had told her all.

"I repaired the tattoo of one of the intruders' females, but I did not mark her. I've never once raised a mortal from the dead. As for this one…" He glared at the shaman. "He never died. Instead he struck a bargain with me for immortality."

"One I sorely regret each time he turns me to ice," the old man said to her.

"Hold your tongue," Cul told him before turning back to her. "Now you reveal your purpose in coming here, wench. Did she send you as a gift? Do you think to mate with me, and produce a clan of halflings? For I cannae breed, even if I wished to fack you."

"By the Gods, who doesnae wish to get me with child this day?" Lilias sighed and rubbed her eyes. "I've no' come to you for that. I'm barren. We also share the same bloodline."

"Ho." The shaman smirked at Cul. "'Twould seem I'm in the right."

"I don't believe you," Cul declared. As she rose from the bench he took a step back. "My warriors will cut you to pieces before you can use your power on me."

"My power doesnae harm." Lilias held up her hands for his scrutiny, and the magic shimmering around them looked as if it had come from sky and sunlight. "It unlocks the past. You remember only your desire for vengeance, Culvar. Permit me show you what more you wished."

She moved so quickly Cul couldn't evade her touch. As soon as her fingers pressed against his face a torrent of images flashed through his thoughts.

Long ago, when he had been forced to resurrect dead mortals for the king, he saw the beautiful Pritani slave open her eyes as he brought her back to life. Rather than despise him like the other mortal females he had resurrected and delivered to the palace, she had been kind. After that she had become the king's favorite, and asked for Cul to attend her. Secretly she had treated him like a son, and taught him her language. From her he'd learned the goodness and compassion that had been denied him by his Sluath kin.

Sometime later Cul was ordered to remove the beautiful slave from the palace, as she had fallen out of favor with the king. Instead of casting her into the slave pits, he took her to the secret chamber he had created in the outer tunnels to keep her safe. As a mortal she could not leave the underworld, however, for attempting to pass through any gate would kill her instantly.

When her belly rapidly swelled Culvar realized the king had gotten her with child.

He remembered finding her writhing in the throes of childbirth. He saw himself attending to her, and wrapping the newborn in his own cloak. He held the slave as she wept over the infant female in despair. He listened to the promises they made to each other as the baby slept in his arms.

Ye shall help me keep her safe when I return to the palace.

You cannot go back to him. The king shall slaughter you.

I made him cast me out, and I shall make him want me again. If I dinnae succeed, then ye must raise and protect her.

Time blurred. True to her word the beautiful slave once more became the king's favorite concubine. Her daughter grew quickly in beauty and charm. Cul saw himself sneaking off to visit the little female, and keeping her company whenever her mother could not slip away from the king. The child had listened to his stories of the mortal realm with wide eyes. When she began to speak he taught her the same language her mother spoke.

She never asked why she wasn't permitted to leave the chamber, or where her mother served, or who Culvar was. He didn't understand why until much later, when she revealed her unique power to him after he'd taken a particularly cruel beating from Iolar.

Dinnae fear, Brother. I shall make gone yer suffering.

You cannae heal me, little one. I'm partly mortal, so 'twill take time.

Yer fear I'll take. She touched his brow, and the bitter dread that he carried faded away, along with his memory of the beating.

Cul soon learned that the child's power had limits. She could only affect one mind at a time. What truly shocked him was when he found her playing skip-stones outside her chamber with one of the guards.

I make him think himself mortal, and me his *sister,* the child had whispered to him. *Go into the chamber, and I make him forget he saw ye.*

Despite her ability to manipulate the mind of anyone she touched, the child rarely strayed far from her secret room. Cul now saw just how much he had done to protect her, but also how the child had helped him. By the time she had grown to a maiden Iolar had inflicted so much suffering on Cul that he might have ended himself, if not for the little halfling slipping into his cell, and holding him with her small hands.

I shall take away your pain as if 'twas never caused, Brother.

He saw every moment that had passed from her birth until the day her mother had told him of Iolar's plot to murder the king so he might seize power. They could not stop the prince, whose hatred was such that as soon as he took the throne he would have them both tortured to death.

Ye must escape the underworld before yer brother ends the king, the beautiful slave told Cul. *Before ye go yer memories of me and the child must be taken from ye, for if ye're caught–*

I understand. I shall do whatever you wish, but I cannae abandon you here.

I'm yet mortal. I would but return to the moment of my death. She looked down at the little girl sleeping in her arms, and kissed the top of her head. *I'll see that she shall come to ye when 'tis safe for her to flee. Vow to me ye will ever protect her.*

Always.

I love ye, lad. Never forget yer vow to me.

Lilias took her hand from Cul's face and held him upright as his shattered leg buckled. She had the strength of a demon, but she smiled as sweetly as a mortal. "'Tis good to see you again, Brother."

"Ye're his *sister*." The old shaman chuckled and shook his head. "Now that I wouldnae reckon, gazing upon ye."

"Sister." Cul clutched at her, astounded and horrified all at once. "Why didn't you come to me before now? What happened after I escaped?"

"Too much to tell you all at once. 'Tis a storm coming, and with that Iolar and the others." She put her arm around him. "If we're to keep the Mag Raith alive, and survive ourselves, we've much to do."

Chapter Twenty-One

AFTER BUILDING UP the fire Domnall gathered the clan in front of the great hall's central hearth to tell them of the secret he had kept for so long. As he spoke Mael produced a bottle of whiskey, which he passed around to the others. Everyone drank, even Rosealise.

Retelling the events that had led to him murdering his own sire proved somewhat easier than he'd expected, although the shame of what he'd done still weighed on him.

"I cannae tell you why Nectan attacked me in my sleep," Domnall admitted once he'd finished his tale. "Mayhap he reckoned I'd try to thwart his bargain and save my brothers from such a fate.

Had I ken what he'd planned, I'd never have left the settlement."

"He likely feared you'd challenge his rule over the decision," Mael said slowly. "As his heir 'twas your right."

"We'll never ken," Domnall told them, and then looked at Kiaran. "Like you I didnae plan to return from the hunt. For killing my sire I'd be put to the blade, and I wished to live. I meant to ride off in the night while the rest of you slept. 'Twas for that I reckoned the Gods damned us."

"Mayhap if we'd no' gone into the fortress, we'd have shared that journey," the falconer said dully.

"I'd like to point out that defending yourself against someone who is trying to kill you in your sleep can't be grounds for damnation," Jenna pointed out. "Nor is thinking about running away from a terrible situation."

"I wouldnae have been sleeping that night," Edane said, his mouth tight as he rubbed a hand over his chest. "My heart, 'twas failing, and I didnae have the strength to hunt anymore. I didnae wish to become the tribe's next shaman. 'Twas why I brought a potion to end my life. I drank the full vial just before we sought refuge in the old fortress."

Nellie rubbed her shoulder against his. "Glad that didn't work, Mister."

Broden stared at him. "I remember. You collapsed, and then–" He stopped and swore as he rubbed his brow. "Fack, but willnae I ever recollect that time without a dagger to the brain?"

Mariena kissed his temple. "There. I make it better, no?" She then drew back and frowned. "It does not transfer to me, the pain you feel. So, it is not from a wound."

"Spell-lash," Edane told her. "'Tisnae as true pain."

Rosealise gently prodded Mael, who took a gulp from his goblet before he said, "I meant to kill my brute of a sire after we returned. I schemed to make it seem a drunken mishap while out hunting grice with him."

"'Twas why you kept setting traps near the cliffs?" Kiaran asked.

"Aye. I meant to shove him over the edge." The big man sighed. "I'd been plotting his end for weeks after he beat my sisters and *máthair* so badly he broke their bones."

"I know something about brutal parents,"

Rosealise said, and twined her fingers through his. "Had I been given the chance, I think I might have done the same to my last employer for sacrificing her daughter to her vanity."

Broden grunted. "I made a trap of myself when I learned that Sileas gave me as a bed slave to the Carrack headman."

"The headman who killed your sire during that raid on your birth tribe?" Edane asked, his voice tight.

"Aye. I promised Sileas I'd go to serve the Carrack after our last hunt." The trapper stared down at the flames. "Only I schemed to cut the headman's throat, and name myself the assassin to his tribe before I ended myself. 'Twould have sent the Carrack seeking vengeance against Sileas and all my sire's tribe."

"Which is why we are nice to you, *mon charmant*," Mariena said in a soothing tone. "You are very lethal when you are angry."

"'Tisnae the same as what I've done," Kiaran said suddenly. "You defended yourself against a murderous sire, Chieftain. Edane, your potion didnae end you. Mael and Broden never carried out their schemes. Taye and her people died because I couldnae hold my tongue. I claimed myself Pritani so you'd welcome me into your tribe. If 'tis for true evil we're damned, then 'tis mine."

"You dinnae ken exactly what I meant to do to the Carrack," Broden told him. "Or the pleasure I felt to imagine his warriors attacking Sileas and my birth tribe."

"I meant to first get my sire drunk," Mael said. "So he couldnae fight me. 'Twas cowardly." He turned toward Edane. "You're certain you didnae die?"

The archer shrugged. "Mayhap the demons brought me back."

"Enough jesting." The falconer stood. "I've confessed, and I'd be judged now. Among the Pritani the punishment for my wrongs, even for a lad, 'twas death."

His stark reminder made everyone fall silent.

"I never took my sire's place, but I'm the last headman of the Mag Raith. As such 'tis my decision." Domnall looked around at the men and women he considered his family. "'Tis as a clan we now live, however, so 'tis how we shall choose. Does Kiaran merit life, or death?"

"Life," Rosealise said instantly. "We've seen enough death, all of us."

"Like so, my lady." Mael showed her how to extend her hand and turn it palm-up in the old gesture for life. To the falconer he said, "Your sire did all the killing of the Pritani. No' you." He then turned his hand up beside his mate's.

"You're an arse with boils," Broden said as he held out his palm. "'Tisnae a reason to die."

"I've got to go with what I know about you," Jenna said and smiled at the falconer. "Like on the way here, when you wrapped me in your cloak to keep me warm?" She showed him her open hand. "That guy deserves to live."

"To choose life, it is the nice change." Mariena held out her palm as she glanced at the chieftain. "But if Domnall ever wants you dead, I will kill you for him. Quickly, of course, as I like you."

"I ken what 'tis to be saddled with an unwanted fate," Edane said slowly, and turned his hand up. "I'd see you survive that."

Shame filled Kiaran's face. "You cannae trust me."

"I don't," Nellie said, a hint of laughter in her voice. She walked up to him and tilted her head back to peer at his pale face. "You've done a lot of wrong, pal. Even if it was for the right reasons, still doesn't let you off the hook." She turned her palm up, and then used it to pat his cheek. "But if I have to live with it, so should you."

The falconer turned to Domnall. "I'm a Viking's bastart, and nearly a demon. Will you wait until I sprout claws and attack your lady before you end me?"

He sounded almost desperate to be slain, which decided it for the chieftain. "Aye, you've wings, but in truth a Sluath would never offer his life to protect us. As for Jenna and our ladies, I'd no' advise you try. They're far from helpless maidens."

His wife grinned. "Damn straight."

"You're our near-demon, Kiaran mag Raith." Domnall held out his hand palm-up. "So shall you live."

As Jenna handed him his sword, the falconer swiped at his eyes. The faint gleam of wetness on his fingers reassured Domnall more than any word Kiaran had uttered.

"Now we must see what we may coax from Lilias," he said.

"Or you may bring her to me," Rosealise said gently. "I dislike using my ability, but the lady already gave me leave to use it on her."

Kiaran sheathed his blade before accompanying Domnall outside. Once away from the rest of the clan, he said, "Lilias and I, we became lovers again, as 'twas in the underworld. She claimed 'twould keep me from changing to Sluath. I tried to refuse her, but when she disrobed and showed all of her beauty to me, I couldnae keep my hands from her."

"You're flesh, no' stone." This new wrinkle would complicate matters, but he felt certain Lilias posed no true threat. "Whatever she claimed, the lass cares for you. We've all seen that. I reckon you feel the same."

A short laugh burst from him. "Gods save me, but I think I love her."

Domnall followed Kiaran into the tower, and mounted the stairs to his aviary. When he hoisted up the panel of bars blocking the passage, he smelled something burnt.

"Hold." He put a hand on the falconer's arm as he drew his sword. "Lilias, show yourself." No reply came, and when Domnall stepped into the aviary he saw why. "She's gone."

"Aye." Kiaran bent down to retrieve a tattered, torn sleeve mottled with dark stains, and knotted it in his fist. "And I ken who took her."

Chapter Twenty-Two

BY THE TIME Mael joined Domnall and Kiaran in their search for Lilias, fierce black clouds mottled the edges of the midday skies. Cooler air from the approaching storm whipped around them as they returned to the tower. Mael felt a judder through his spine every time lightning streaked through the burgeoning tempest, which now appeared to be stretching across the horizon in every direction.

"'Tis as when we first entered the old fortress," the chieftain said as he pulled aside the old tartan. "Odd that for all our wrongs, none of us became Sluath in truth."

"Mayhap we should inspect our trapper's

spine," Mael joked, and saw Kiaran bristle. "I but jest, Brother."

"I ken you do. 'Tis only that I reckon Broden's friendship kept me from turning entire." The falconer's jaw tightened as he glanced at the stairs. "As did Lilias's affections. Where did that monstrous fack take her?"

"We shall find her," Domnall assured him. "If we must pull down the walls of the stronghold."

Despite the chieftain's promise Mael found no tracks leading from the aviary other than the falconer's, and no trace of the lady at all. It seemed as if she had walked through the walls, as the chieftain's mate could when she used her ability. Mael then employed his own power, which allowed his senses to stretch far beyond any mortal could detect. He caught the faintest trace of Lilias's scent, and followed it outside. It led him to the outer wall of the hedge maze.

"Earlier she fell from her mount into the juniper," Kiaran said as he and Domnall flanked him. "I pulled her out and took her into the tower, and you ken the rest."

"'Mayhap she escaped the watcher, and ran past," Mael glanced around them before he regarded the chieftain. "I'll walk the hedge border to see if she followed it into the forest."

Domnall nodded. "Kiaran and I shall ride out to the river and patrol the barrier. Take Edane with you."

Mael went into the stronghold to summon the archer, whom he found with Rosealise. Upon hearing the chieftain's order, she insisted on accompanying them both to survey the lethal living trap. Edane took a lit torch from a stanchion as they passed.

"I do not possess many fond memories of this labyrinth," Rosealise told her husband as they walked alongside the archer. "Especially as it tried to kill us both. Yet as terrible as it was to fall naked out of the sky into the trap, at least I landed on you, my love."

"But for that I'd have burned the facking thing to the ground," Mael assured her as he kissed her cheek.

"Mayhap you willnae be obliged to." Edane stopped and held up his torch to illuminate a darker section. "Look here. 'Tis dying."

Mael tugged his wife back from the spreading patch of withering juniper. Using his sight gift, he saw the shimmer of magic slowly dimming from the hedge as well. "The enchantment also fades, Brother."

The archer stretched out his hand, moving it along the dying plants. "By the Gods, so 'tis. The magic used to animate the hedges, 'tis been dispelled by another power." His brow furrowed. "No' Pritani or Druid or Sluath. I've never felt the like."

"There's something more, my dear sir." Rosealise pointed to the ground. "This may be the spot where Lilias fell from her horse. Look at the hoof ruts in the soil here."

"Aye." The archer reached out, hesitating for a moment before he grasped one of the thorny canes and snapped it off. It crumbled to dust on his palm before sifting away on the breeze. "The hedge, 'tisnae dying. 'Tis aging."

"Stand back, my lady," Mael said, drawing his sword as Edane did the same.

Once Rosealise had moved away, the two men hacked at the hedge with their blades. The wall exploded into a shower of dust over them, as if the juniper had been dead for so long it had completely rotted.

"Egad." Rosealise removed her apron and used it to wipe the debris from their faces.

"You will both need a thorough bathe tonight."

Edane murmured his thanks, while Mael used his torch to examine the wide gap in the hedge. On the other side a large rectangular recess stretched out on the ground, with a narrow set of steps that led down below the surface. When he used his ability, he could see through the blackness within the hole to a trio of figures coming out of the passage.

"Wife, go and fetch Broden and Mariena," Mael said, keeping his voice low as he signaled danger to the archer. Edane nodded, drew his bow and shifted to the opposite side of the gap.

"I, too, know what that gesture means, my darling," Rosealise said, making no move to leave them.

"Then heed me, my lady," Mael told her.

His mate instead raised her reed whistle to her lips, and blew it sharply three times. She then picked up a large stone from the ground and joined him. When he scowled at her, she frowned back. "You will not send me away at such a moment. Whatever comes, we must face it together."

"You're as stubborn as–" Mael gaped as he

saw Lilias climb up out of the recess. "By the Gods. 'Tis the lass."

The Pritani woman immediately turned to aid the hobbling figure behind her. Mael heard Edane mutter something, and then he saw Lilias smile at the old man she'd helped out. He wore the garb of a Pritani shaman, and possessed such long silver-white hair the ends trailed on the ground.

Since neither appeared to pose much threat, and the rest of the clan would soon arrive, Mael decided to step out and confront them. "'Tis good to see you unharmed, Lady Lilias, but you've some explaining to do. What do you here? Who's this old fellow?"

"As oft as ye brought yer sisters and *máthair* for me to tend their hurts," the elderly man said, "I'd reckon ye'd remember, son of Fargas."

"Master Ewan?" Edane gasped. The archer's jaw dropped.

"Aye, in the flesh, such 'tis." His gaze shifted and his expression changed to delight. "Ah, here ye be, my unwilling apprentice. 'Tis good to see ye again, lad. Never reckoned I'd ken the pleasure after all this time."

"You're our tribe's shaman." Mael glanced at

the archer, who lowered his bow as if to confirm that. "How?"

"Ah, much studying of spells and potions, and a skill for wielding magic." Ewan nodded at the gaping Edane. "Or do ye mean how came I here?"

"You cannae yet live." Edane's hand trembled as he reached out to touch the old man's shoulder. "'Tis been too long, and you mortal."

"I followed ye to this place," the old man said. "And found the tunnels beneath, and the beast. We parlayed so that I might wait for ye." He pulled up the sleeve of his tunic to show the Sluath ink on his wrinkled forearm.

The moment the archer's fingers brushed the shaman's tattoo he dropped to his knees, and touched his brow to a gnarled hand. "Forgive me, Master."

"I'd beg the same of ye," Ewan said as he tugged him to his feet. "How well we must amuse the Gods, that they willnae be rid of us." He embraced him, and then turned toward the recess. "Ye cannae go on skulking in the shadows forever, ye great beast. Come and show yerself to my kin."

As the hulking figure of a crippled demon

limped up the steps Mael pushed his wife and Lilias behind him, and Edane did the same with the shaman. "Rosealise, take them and run to the stronghold, *now*."

"I shall do no such thing," his lady said, sounding highly indignant. "Really, my dear husband, you must cease demanding I leave you in peril."

"Watcher." Edane drew two more arrows and fitted them alongside the one notched in his bow. "'Twill be a pleasure to put you back in the ground, you vicious fack."

"He shallnae harm you again, any of you," Lilias said as she stepped between the halfling demon and them. "Culvar wishes but to make peace with your clan."

Horses whinnied behind them, and Domnall and Kiaran dismounted and ran to join them, their blades held ready. Broden and Mariena emerged from the forest at a flat run, and took attack positions.

"Hello, Monster." Nellie stepped out of the shadows. "We need to talk about that wall you dropped on me and my snuggleup." Daggers appeared in both of her small hands. "Or maybe not."

"Step aside, lass," Kiaran said. His kestrels gathered to hover over his head, their dark eyes fixed on the watcher. "He's mine."

"He did save my life," Mariena put in. "But only so he might use my power on himself. Of course, I could end your pain right now." She brandished a long, thin blade.

"Stop it," Jenna shouted, rushing through the men in her wraith form. As everyone glared at her she materialized beside the chieftain and threw out her arms. "Can we hold off on the fighting for a second, and hear what Lilias has to say? Then you can hack them to pieces with a clear conscience."

Domnall's nostrils flared, but he gave a curt nod, and signaled his warriors to stay in their positions.

"A pretty wench, but she speaks a strange tongue," the shaman said to Edane before he bowed to the chieftain's wife. "Fair day, my lady. 'Twas a neat ruse, to make yerself seem spirit. Ye must teach me that one."

"Uh, hey, there." Jenna bobbed an awkward curtsey in return. "I'm American. It's a long story. Welcome to Dun Chaill."

"A pleasure to meet ye, lass." The old man

gave Culvar a sour look. "Unlike the others."

"Okay." The architect regarded Lilias. "Whatever you have to say, you'd better talk fast. Right now."

"I can do better than speak, my lady." Lilias turned to the falconer. "You wished the truth from me, Kiaran. With my brother's aid, I shall give that to you and your clan."

The watcher took hold of her hand, and their bodies began to glow. Mael felt a moment of utter shock before the golden-blue light swept out and engulfed him and the clan.

SHE SOMETIMES THOUGHT of herself as one of the curses hurled at her by the other enslaved: *Coward. Whore. Traitor.* The demons called her Treasure, however, and that was the name she answered to. She wanted them to think her as precious and irreplaceable as Prince Iolar did, so they wouldn't discover she was more like them than the mortals.

Halflings born to slaves in the underworld rarely lived longer than a few moments. Those that survived ended strangled or smothered by their insane mothers, or killed while being used as a torment by their sadistic sires. She and two others had been the only exceptions, but she had been hidden away for years. As for Culvar, he had been tormented for so long it had nearly driven him insane before he escaped.

The only way Treasure could discover if he had survived in the mortal realm would be to do the same. And she would do it, but for the fear.

Creeping through the tunnels meant keeping her footfalls as silent as Treasure could. Each time she ventured away from the palace she risked exposing herself to the sentries and patrols. All Sluath knew how much Iolar prized her, and that he never allowed her to go unescorted anywhere in the underworld. If the guards found her alone, they wouldn't harm her. Yet if they knocked her out before she could touch them…

'Tis but fear that makes ye a slave. No' them.

As always, hearing her mother's voice whisper inside her mind made Treasure feel a little braver. She'd never be as strong or determined as the blurry, beautiful memory of that valiant lady, but she still carried a reminder of her fierce love. As she curled her hand around the carved pendant that she wore, the terrible guilt rose inside her. Her mother had sacrificed her own life to keep her safe after convincing her to make an impossible vow.

As soon as I may, I shall escape to the mortal realm, Máthair, and find my brother, and go to the druids. I shall tell them of the underworld, and the Sluath, and how they may stop them from culling mortals forever.

The only problem with Treasure keeping that promise was she had yet to find the courage to step through one of the gates. Each time she approached, the uncertainties that plagued her began shrieking in her head.

You know nothing of your nature. What if passing through it kills you? What awaits you on the other side? Will you still have your power? What if the Pritani decide you are their enemy? How will you defend yourself against more than one?

Of course, then came the worst, which always turned her back from her chance at freedom.

What if they discover what you've done?
Coward.

She had promised her mother that she would escape, but she hadn't said when. At first she believed she could leave any time she wished. Then she had been caught by more than one guard, which made it impossible to use her power to free herself. They had brought her to the prince, who had demanded to know how she was alive. She had used her power on him to remove the memories of her mother, and keep him from hurting her. That had only resulted in her being locked up in his treasure chamber.

Sometimes Treasure felt glad her mother was dead, so she couldn't see what her daughter had done to stay alive.

Soon she'd have to return to the palace. The intense gratification provided by the first of the newly-arrived souls from each cull never lasted very long. Once Iolar used the prettiest and youngest he'd send for her. The prince always made her listen to his exploits in the mortal realm, regaling her with every repulsive detail. Then he would seize her to reach into her mind, for he believed that, through her thoughts, she gave him the greatest pleasure any Sluath had ever known.

Treasure stayed alive because she used her power to alter Iolar's memories to make him believe that.

It had disgusted her at first, but now she sensed it had gone on too long. Everything about her that remained mortal had been slowly fading away. Fear of her power being discovered was the only thing Treasure felt any more. Even Nellie, her only companion in the prince's treasure room, had noticed how cold she'd become.

You've got to find something to hold onto, Sister. If you don't, and soon, you're going to lose what's left of your human half.

Just before Treasure reached the outmost gate, the sound of it opening made her go still. She'd watched to be sure all the demons had returned from the last culling before she'd slipped out of the palace. Iolar never permitted any stragglers. Could it be the outcast? Why would Culvar risk his life to come back? The prince would kill him the moment he caught sight of him, and everything her mother had done would be for nothing.

Terror streaked through Treasure as she darted across the tunnel to conceal herself in a pool of shadows.

Blue-white power arced across the tunnel, and then four large, dirty, muscular males emerged. *No, five.* One of the men carried the body of another over his broad shoulder.

Treasure's eyes widened as she watched the gate's magic settling over them in a cascade of lethal light. She couldn't help covering her face with her trembling hands. She didn't want to see them burned to ash. Any moment they would begin screaming, and the stench of burnt flesh would fill the tunnels, and bring the guards running.

Any moment.

No sound came from the men, and the feel of magic in the air subsided. Treasure peeked through her fingers to see the now-glowing figures of the tribesmen. Instead of snuffing out their lives, the power slid down their bodies and pooled around their fur boots before it sank into the stone and vanished.

That was almost worse to behold. It meant they were no longer mortal.

"'Tis somehow enchanted," a tall one with stern features said as he scanned the tunnels, his mouth tight. He sniffed the air. "Another watches us."

"One of those facking druids, hoping to snare Romans." The second man, who appeared even more beautiful than a demon, gestured back toward the arch. "We're caught."

"Aye, but Edane's breathing better now." The largest of the five carefully lowered the thin body he carried onto the stone. "Lad, can ye open yer eyes?"

"Dinnae try to rouse him." The fourth man

came out of the shadows, his flesh smooth and golden, his face like none of the others. Small, fierce-looking birds clung to his shoulders and arms. His dark blue eyes glittered tiny white glints from the magic that still infused him. More gleamed in the long, red-gold hair streaming over his wide shoulders and broad chest.

"Why no', Kiaran?" the bigger man asked.

"Listen." His eyes abruptly darkened as he nodded past them. "They come for us."

Behind the man with the birds, the enchanted rock began to change. Treasure knew that it formed itself based on the secret terror of the humans brought into the underworld. Gore and blood spattered the image of a brute of a man with long white-gold hair. He swung a huge sword as if to behead the Kiaran.

But Treasure could not stop staring at the man with the birds. Since the living rock had changed, that meant somehow he still remained partly mortal.

Could he be a halfling, like her?

The sound of the approaching guards grew louder. She could not save all five men, for it would take too much time to explain their situation to them. If she had to use her power, it would only work on one at a time. She might be able to conceal Kiaran and his birds if she could separate him from the others before the guards came.

I'll take him to the hidden chamber where Fiana kept me.

Treasure pushed aside her fear, and moved out into the light.

Chapter Twenty-Three

❧

A LIGHT RAIN began to fall as Lilias focused on the bespelled clan. Drawing on her brother's magic to augment her own, she removed the last of the memory locks she had placed in their minds. Restoring their forgotten time in the underworld took only a few moments, thanks to the pervasive strength of combining her magic with Culvar's.

"Before you release them," Culvar muttered, his tone sullen, "you should remove all knowledge of your sire from their minds. They will not forgive you for being half-demon, or the spawn of the Sluath king."

"I'm done with hiding and deceiving." Once she had finished giving back the clan's memories, she withdrew her power from their minds. "I've missed you so, Brother."

"I never thought once of you. When I first saw you the day you came, I thought you were your mother." When she would have released his hand, he held onto hers. "Why did you leave me with that one memory of Fiana coming to my cell, and giving me the map to Dun Chaill?"

Lilias sighed. "She didnae wish you to ever forget the vow you made."

Culvar let go of her hand, and their entwined power slowly dispersed.

It gladdened Lilias to see all of the men slowly lower their weapons. As the magic faded the clan's newly-awakened awareness showed in expressions of astonishment, joy, and relief.

"Treasure." Nellie flung herself at Lilias and wrapped her in a close embrace. "Golly, Sister, why didn't you tell us who you were when you got here?"

"Forgive me, Helen." Being held by her old friend made raw emotion well up inside Lilias. "'Twas necessary to veil nearly all your memories of me."

"You're the only reason we escaped the underworld," Jenna reminded her before kissing her cheek. "Consider yourself my best friend forever."

Domnall came to her, and dropped down on one knee. "My thanks, Princess. We owe you our lives."

The chieftain had always insisted on calling her that during their time in the underworld, as if she were royalty instead of a slave. It made Lilias wish she could cry like a mortal.

"Your clan brought me out of darkness, Domnall." She urged him to his feet. "Forgive me for making you believe a Sluath helped you escape. I ken 'twas confusing."

"I worried we'd be recaptured by the Sluath here," Edane said thoughtfully. "'Twas my notion to have you alter our memories to recall you only as a faceless demon traitor."

"Yet you also made us forget each other," Mariena put in, sounding annoyed. "And separated us across time."

"It was because of the stream," Jenna guessed. "I remember now. Treasure said only the Sluath could freely travel time through it."

"And the rotten henge?" Mael asked, rain droplets leaving clean tracks on his ashy hands.

"You fell from your horse there," Rosealise said to Lilias, before she could answer him.

Lilias nodded. "Aye, my blood spilt and–"

"Soaked into the earth to end my enchantment," Culvar finished.

As everyone began to talk at once, the chieftain bent his head and asked in a voice only for her ears, "Before you departed the underworld, Princess, kept you your vow to me?"

Her smile faded, and she nodded. "'Tis done."

He closed his eyes for a moment before he turned to the old shaman. "Master Ewan. By the Gods, 'tis truly you."

As the two men clasped arms, Lilias braved a look at Kiaran. He stood watching her as if she'd stolen his memories again instead of restoring them. When she took a step toward him, he shook his head and moved away.

She stopped where she was, as her heart sank and her chest clenched. He knew about the love they had found together while in the underworld. It had not only kept him from transforming, but had given her the courage to conquer her fears. They had saved his brothers and their ladies, and escaped to freedom, just as they had planned. He even knew why she had done everything as she had. She couldn't understand why he regarded her as a stranger now.

'Tis as if he's no' the same Kiaran I loved, Lilias thought, and then it struck her: the time difference. For her their escape had been only a few days past.

For her lover, it had been more than ten centuries.

"Enough. We shall talk inside," Domnall said as he glanced up at the sky, and then eyed Culvar. "For the princess's sake I shallnae end you this day. Crawl back into your hole in the dirt. We shall meet again."

The halfling stiffened. "It is more than a hole, intruder, and Dun Chaill is *my* castle."

Edane raised his bow. ""Twill be your grave, then."

"'Tisnae his fault, what Culvar did," Lilias said quickly. "'Tis mine. My *máthair* made me take from him all memories of us, to protect me. With them he lost all the goodness and mercy she taught him. He came here with only hatred of the Sluath, and the desire to avenge the suffering he endured in the underworld."

"Indeed." Domnall appeared unmoved. "We've borne as much at his hands."

"You powered the traps here with your magic, and control the many iron warriors here?" Mariena asked Culvar, who nodded. She regarded the chieftain. "I do not like it any more than you do, *monsieur*, but he has value to us."

"More than ye ken, lad," the old shaman said to Domnall.

The rain grew heavier and colder as swelling black clouds crept toward the sun.

"'Twould be grand to warm my old bones by a real hearth," Ewan said to no one in particular. "And I'd no' refuse a hot brew, should a kind soul offer a cup."

Domnall eyed Culvar for another long moment before he said, "Very well. I shall hear how you wish to make peace. Mael, Broden, keep him between you, and your blades ready."

The trapper and the seneschal drew their swords and flanked the halfling as Broden said, "Aye, Chieftain."

Chapter Twenty-Four

LIGHTNING JABBED AT the ridges in bright, thin jags of white around Galan. It smashed the rock and set small fires to the wilting greenery. When a particularly powerful strike caused a stunted oak's trunk to explode, nearly all the Sluath fled into the caves.

"Perhaps you should save that for the rebels, my liege," Danar suggested from beneath the stone outcropping he'd occupied.

As he poured his power and the prince's into swelling the storm, Galan could feel Iolar's weakness diminishing. The prince thought he could steal his power without notice, but he'd expected as much from the canny Sluath. It worked in his favor for the prince to regard him as a crazed, unaware fool. To lay proper siege to Dun Chaill he needed Iolar and his demons. They also knew nothing of the many traps Culvar had waiting for them inside the stronghold.

Aye, Culvar awaits.

Galan would have to take him alive along with Fiana. From the halfling he would learn all the secrets of the underworld. Once he learned how to travel through time as they did, then he would return to the day of Ruadri's birth. The prospect of being able to go back and strangle his newborn son before he drew his first breath made him laugh.

As for Fiana, he would assure that while she would forever wish herself dead again, she would never die.

At last high, heavy black clouds blotted out the sky in every direction, and the rising wind turned cutting with curtains of frozen rain. The loss of sunlight plunged the highlands into a darkness beyond that of night. Yet as Galan separated his power from the prince's, he saw every live thing glow as if lit from within.

The demons did not need sunlight, it seemed, to hunt in the mortal realm.

"That should suffice," Iolar said. "We'll be

able to fly for days, if not weeks." His eyes glowed with satisfied malevolence as he spread his wings. "All you need do now is lead us to the rebels once night falls."

The prince's smugness, like the tiny bits of sleet pelting them both, had no weight to it. Yet as Danar looked out at them from his temporary shelter, Galan thought on how often the second protected Iolar. He also remembered the pleasure the big demon had taken in clawing out his throat.

He pointed to Danar. "First you give that one to me."

The prince uttered an uneasy chuckle. "You cannot cull a demon, Aedth. We don't have souls like mortals. Really, must I explain everything about the Sluath to–"

Galan back-handed Iolar, who went hurtling into the side of the slope. As he stalked toward the outcropping, Danar stepped out to meet him, his face ashen and his claws clotted with frost. A moment before he reached him the big demon went down on his knees, flung his head back, and spread his arms wide.

"So spineless you willnae face me, then?" Galan said, bending down to look into his dull eyes. "Beg me for your life, and I may spare you."

"Why should I? You want me dead, and you're wise to be rid of me," Danar said, his expression calm. "I've tormented you many times, and enjoyed ending your mortal life. You could never trust me, not after what the prince commanded me to do to you."

A shard of ice slid from the demon's eye down his cheek like a frozen tear.

"You're quick to shift blame on Iolar." Galan gripped Danar's massive jaw, enjoying the feel of the cold Sluath blood trickling down his new claws.

"As long as he rules the horde, I am his creature, as are the others." The big demon smiled at him. "He's using you again, Aedth, and not just for all the power you've attained. Once he has what he desires from you, he'll order me to take your head—and I will."

"Traitor," Iolar yelled. He scrambled up, hurried over, and kicked a swath of mud at the big demon's face. "It was you all along, wasn't it? You helped the rebels escape, and sealed off the gates to the underworld. Now you dare try to goad our new brother into attacking me."

Galan ignored the prince's ranting. "As long as he rules?" he asked the big demon softly.

Danar nodded. "After I became Sluath, I swore loyalty forever to he who rules. We have no honor, but among us only death can sever such an oath." He glanced at Iolar. "Even when made to one who ripped out *my* throat."

Galan leaned close, and caressed the demon's face with the tips of his claws, scoring his pallid flesh. "Your death, or his?"

Lightning flashed, and a huge bolt rammed through the clouds over their heads.

"You choose." Danar closed his eyes. "I'm too weary to care."

"Choose after the battle," the prince said quickly. When both of them regarded him, he added, "You burned most of the horde back in the village. If we are to prevail over the Mag Raith, we need every Sluath left alive." He sneered at his second. "Even one as traitorous as this blade-riddled lump."

"My prince," Meirneal said as he dragged the battered body of a mortal female behind him. He scanned their faces before he said, "I only wished to ask, have you finished with this one?"

"What?" Iolar scowled at him. "Yes, why?"

"I'll get rid of the body." He licked his lips before displaying the tiny, dingy pearls of his teeth. "Eventually."

Galan stood and stretched out his claws, catching the next bolt of lightning that sizzled down from the sky. He gathered it into a ball, which he flung at the corpse. Meirneal screamed shrilly as the white-blue flames that consumed the mortal raced up the sleeve of his pastel tunic, setting it alight.

"I said, we need every Sluath," Iolar said and cast a swath of ice over the small demon's burning arm, extinguishing the fire. Then he placed another over his screeching mouth, silencing him. "Even the most repulsive have their uses. Imagine our little Meirneal slowly dining on one of your enemies, once he heals, of course."

As Meirneal writhed, clutching his scorched limb, Galan could feel pain radiating from him like a stench of rot. It did nothing for the knotted hollow that had been growing in his gut since he'd climbed out of the pit. Yet starved as he felt, another part of him swelled with a different hunger as he watched the childlike Sluath's suffering. He wanted to do the same thing to the Mag Raith, one by one, and then violate them in countless, imaginative ways as they screamed from the agony of their wounds.

They cannae die. They heal from every injury.

If he were careful, he could go on hurting them for as long as he chose. Galan thought of Broden, whose slut of a mother had been a bedslave.

"After the battle," he told the prince, "you shall give me rule over all the Sluath."

"Yes, of course." Iolar waved away the acrid smoke coming from the burning corpse. "You deserve the throne, Prince Galan."

"King." He watched hatred flicker through the prince's golden eyes. "I shall be *King* Aedth to you."

"You sound so much like my father," Iolar said. "Only he was a very bad king. You will make a magnificent ruler." He took hold of Meirneal by his unburned arm. "Come along. You can wrap up that arm with Seabhag's cloak."

"Tell the others to make ready," Galan called after them. "We leave for Dun Chaill once night falls." He glanced at the big demon. "Get up."

Danar lumbered to his feet, and wiped the blood from his face on his sleeve before he bowed low. "When you take the throne, I will become your creature, Aedth."

"All of you shall," he told him, already bored with his fawning.

The big demon nodded. "Then you may command me to take the prince's head—and I will."

Chapter Twenty-Five

KIARAN BROUGHT HALF his kestrels into the stronghold, and sent the others to perch at the castle's highest points to watch for the Sluath. While the ladies brought food and brew for the old shaman, the men of the clan surrounded Culvar. The halfling demon's ruined leg made him clumsy and slow, and when he tried to brace his back against a wall Domnall shoved a bench from the trestle table at him.

"Sit there," he told Culvar, whose walking stick shook as he lowered himself.

Kiaran couldn't keep his gaze long from Lilias, who now wrapped old Ewan in a warm tartan as he hovered near the hearth. Every notion he'd had of her had been shattered by the flood of memories she'd poured into his mind.

Now he knew the sweet, gentle beauty he'd rescued from the flowery meadow had been sired by the Sluath king, and spent her entire life in the underworld. She possessed a power that allowed her to meddle with both mortal and Sluath minds. She'd used it on him, the other hunters, their ladies, and even on her half-brothers, Culvar and Iolar.

Somehow she had made Kiaran love her as well.

Kiaran knew better than to love. He'd seen his mother's desperate love for him—her wild hope to see him free and living among the Pritani—get her killed.

Despite Lilias's claim to have returned all their memories, many questions still plagued him. She had been born of a mortal mother, but never once spoke of the lady. What had happened to the Pritani slave who had given birth to her?

Then, too, Lilias had been in control of the device that had allowed them to escape through the cloud stream. So why had she so cruelly separated his brothers from their mates? How could any female with a heart take from eight lovers all memory of each other?

Kiaran didn't realize he'd voiced his thoughts aloud until everyone fell silent. As Nellie scowled in his direction, Lilias left the old shaman huddled in Broden's whittling chair and came to stand before him.

"You couldnae come back to the mortal realm together," she told him in a voice husky with sadness. "You and your brothers werenae wholly changed to demons. That prevented you from attaining all their powers, and the ability to move through the stream. 'Twould only transport you as mortals, back to your time."

"We didnae return to the tribe or our settlement," Edane said. "We landed in the ash grove of a druid tribe's settlement."

Mael nodded. "Aye, and when we awoke, a hundred years had passed since we'd vanished. We'd become a legend."

"Time doesnae move as quickly in the underworld. A century had passed in the mortal realm by the time you returned. I couldnae change that," she admitted. "As for the place, 'twas the only spot where the magic would shield you from the Sluath."

"Thank the Gods for that, lass," the old shaman called to her. "They'd have found an empty settlement." He yawned and his eyelids drooped. "Or angry Romans."

Rosealise looked perplexed as she came to stand with them. "If mortals may only return to their time as you say, then shouldn't we ladies have arrived in the future?"

"You didnae come as the men to the underworld," Lilias said as the other women gathered around them. "The Sluath culled you. The stream, 'twould only return you to that very place and moment in your time."

"When the demons took our ladies, near death," Domnall murmured.

"Aye, Chieftain. 'Tis why the Sluath ever seek out mortals in such straits. To be rid of slaves they drive mad, they send them back to their time." She touched the housekeeper's arm. "You'd fallen grave sick, too, my friend. Even if you'd overcome your wounds from the attack you suffered, still you wouldnae long live."

"Yes," Rosealise said, her eyes gleaming with tears. "My poor charge died within weeks from the same disease that afflicted me."

"An entire building had collapsed on top of

me," Jenna said, shuddering. "Nellie had just been shot multiple times in that speakeasy. Mariena, you were bleeding to death in Gestapo headquarters. None of us would have made it."

"Jeepers, I had more holes in me than a Swiss cheese," Edane's mate told her. "I'd have definitely gone to the Big Sleep pronto."

The Frenchwoman sighed. "Given what the Butcher had planned for me, I am very glad you chose not to send us back. Still, I do not understand all of it. Why did you alter our tattoos to give us powers, and make us immortal?"

"The powers I meant to help you once you escaped," Lilias said. "The glyphs keep you alive while frozen in the underworld. Here they bestow immortality when you die a mortal death. Culvar taught me how to alter the ink to bestow abilities."

"How could we come to fourteenth century Scotland," Nellie asked, "and why did we arrive at different times?"

"More than one entering the cloud stream would kill either or both. 'Twas only one other time and place where I could send the four of you: here." Lilias glanced at Culvar for a moment. "Dun Chaill, 'twas ever open to the stream. 'Twas where my *máthair* sent my brother when he escaped."

"I do not know why it remains open," Culvar said as all eyes turned to him. "It simply does."

"Beast," the old shaman muttered as he dozed.

"Why should you help us, Princess?" Kiaran demanded, unable to keep from sneering Domnall's pet name for her. "You'd no reason to leave your coddled position among the demons. The prince adorned you as a queen."

"You have no idea what that evil palooka did to her." Nellie's expression darkened, and she balled her small hands into fists. "So, can it, pal."

"No," Lilias said. "He's right, my friend. You remember how 'twas for us before the Mag Raith came. You ever had to play your part as Nellie, and I'd grown so cold." Lilias lifted her chin as she met his gaze. "When I saw you in the tunnels, Kiaran, you made me yearn to feel again."

"Feel what?" He took hold of her shoulders. "Worshipped? Cherished? Silk on your flesh, pearls in your hair? Desired you feasts of delicacies, and armies of quivering mortal slaves to serve you? Or mayhap that wouldnae satisfy you."

He flung his hand toward the clan. "Even now, each of us would call you *sweet and gentle*."

She cringed but held her ground. "Aye, 'tis my doing, the clan's memory of me thus, but only to protect myself. I couldnae think of—"

"For protection? Or do you feed on their pain like your demon brothers? Did you feed on *mine*? 'Tis why the memory of the day my *máthair* died remains lost to me?"

Lilias's eyes turned a blazing gold. "That you did to yourself, Warrior." She wrenched free of his hands, and hurried off into the kitchens.

Domnall stepped in his path when Kiaran started to follow her. "You're wrong about the princess. Aside from the lady saving this clan, she saw to it you kept your miserable hide intact."

"I dinnae care what she put in your head," he told him.

The chieftain pushed him back. "You dinnae recall that she hid you from the demons? So well did she protect you that never once did you suffer torments at their hands."

"If ever 'twas as you recall," he countered, throwing out his arms. "With her power she can make us believe whatever she wishes."

Nellie marched up to him and prodded his

chest with a finger. "She did all this for *you*, you rube. While you were in hiding, you kept pestering Lilias about the other men until she started taking messages to them for you. You convinced her she could help us escape through time travel in the cloud stream, the only way us mortal ladies could leave. Even when it meant she might be caught, exposed, and killed, she did whatever you wanted."

"Why would she risk so much for a stranger?" Kiaran demanded.

Nellie gave him a pitying look. "Pretty Boy's right. You really are an ass with boils." She stalked off into the kitchens.

Kiaran saw how the halfling demon regarded him, and his anger swelled. "You've something to say to me?"

"I imagined that my sister wished but to feel love again." Culvar leaned back against the wall, his expression smug. "She only ever had me and her mother. We'd cherished her, and protected her, but then we had to leave her behind, knowing neither of us could return."

He felt like kicking the halfling until his good leg snapped. "Loneliness compelled her to help me? 'Tis what you wish me believe? Just how lonely could she feel?"

"Fool." His golden eyes glittered with contempt. "Before you came through that gate, she had been alone for a thousand years."

Chapter Twenty-Six

AS THE CHIEFTAIN issued terse orders to his men, Cul watched three of the females retreat into the kitchen, doubtless to comfort Lilias. The falconer stalked off into the passage leading to the rebuilt tower, followed by the big seneschal, while the trapper and archer went after the females. Silencing Kiaran's suspicions had provided Cul with a little sour satisfaction, but his amusement didn't last. As Domnall and Mariena spoke in low tones, he noted both casting swift glances at him.

Determining his usefulness to the clan would come next.

All that kept him from opening a portal and lurching into it were the memories his sister had unveiled. He understood why her mother had ordered her to take all knowledge of his secret family from him, for if he had been caught by the Sluath during his escape they would have forced it from him. But without that knowledge, his Sluath side ran rampant, even now. He had forever forfeited the gifts of love Fiana and her daughter had bestowed on him, but for their sake he would try to make amends to the Mag Raith.

Then, perhaps with Lilias's help, he would end it all.

The chieftain pulled another bench in front of him, but not to perch on. He reached down and took hold of Cul's ruined leg, and lifted it carefully to prop it on the empty bench.

"You ken that our lady war master cannae heal you," Domnall said. "Yet Edane possesses potions that may ease your pain. Help us, and we shall do the same."

"I have him for that," Cul said, nodding at the sleeping shaman. "What is it that you want of me?"

On the other side of the bench the chieftain unrolled the map scroll Cul had used to lure Rosealise into the vine trap. He then drew his dagger and tapped the intricate drawing.

"You built Dun Chaill from the old fortress where we took shelter." He moved his dagger to the lowest point on the map. "When first we came, we found our way below, to the tunnels, where the demons captured us. 'Tis beneath us now, the Sluath underworld?"

Cul shook his head. "I dug the tunnels under the fortress long before I began work on the upper levels. You and your men stumbled through one of my open entries, and then passed through a portal I created that took you to the underworld. The kingdom of the Sluath does not exist in this realm."

"Then where is it?" Mariena asked, leaning closer. "You were born there, no? And lived much of your life as a slave to the demons. You must have some idea."

"It doesn't matter. It cannot be reached unless you journey there by gate." He bared his jagged teeth in a twisted smile. "Do you wish to visit it again? You didn't fare so well among the Sluath the last time."

"We wish to understand the nature of such." Domnall straightened and looked down at the floor around them. "This portal you created under the old fortress, 'tis yet below?"

"Oh, yes. It's the only gate left that leads to the underworld," Cul said, feeling smug. "I've sealed or destroyed all the others. If the Sluath wish to return to their home, they must now come to Dun Chaill."

"'Tis as you and Broden suspected," the chieftain said to Mariena.

"What is that?" Cul demanded.

"These traps you created with your magic," the Frenchwoman said as she picked up the scroll and rolled it. "You never meant them for mortals. They are for the demons."

"Of course, they are." He felt a surge of contempt. "Why do you think I've devoted centuries building my beautiful castle, and filling it with such delights? For the killing of mortals? I'm not a demon."

Domnall's expression darkened. "You're half-blood, and 'tis a hoard mound in the forest that calls you liar a thousand times."

"I've slain those who came too close, or tried to steal from me," Cul corrected. "Some, like the Romans, even tried to lay claim to my castle. I especially enjoyed slaughtering such greedy simpletons. Dun Chaill was never intended for anyone but me and the Sluath."

"How did you plan to lure them here?" Mariena asked.

"In the beginning I caught some wayward mortals to use as bait, but I found a better use for them. Your clan should serve now." Cul leaned back against the wall, and took comfort from the feel of the smooth stone against his colder flesh. "I have but to lower the spell barrier, and the demon horde will sense us. That will draw them into the castle, where they will fall prey to my traps as they search. I will let them live long enough to know when I destroy the last gate."

The chieftain and the Frenchwoman exchanged another telling look, and then retreated from the hall. Bemused at being left alone, Cul started to rise, and then saw Broden, Lilias and Domnall's mate walk out of the kitchens. The women carried long pieces of flat-sided wood, leather straps, and a bundle of cloth strips.

"You intend to beat me with those?" Cul asked as Jenna placed the wood on the bench in front of him.

"No, Brother." Lilias sat down beside him. "'Tis to help with your leg."

Broden positioned himself against the opposite wall like a sentry.

The chieftain's wife eyed him before she took one piece of wood and placed it alongside his crippled limb.

"I don't have any plaster to make a cast," Jenna told him, "and the Pritani treatment for broken bones won't work on you, so I'm going to splint your leg. Lilias will wrap it. If you cause trouble, then Broden will take over."

The trapper gave him an unpleasant smile.

Cul decided not to resist, and watched his sister hold the wood in place as the American began strapping the pieces on either side of his limb. "You are surprisingly forgiving. You know that I lured you into the armory with those gems so that my iron warriors would kill you."

Jenna made a vague affirmative sound as she slid a strap up over his knee.

"'Tis my doing as much as yours," Lilias said as she picked up the linen, and began winding it around the contraption. "Had you memories of our life together, you wouldnae have done thus."

"We had no life in the underworld," he told her, his anger rising. "We're neither mortal nor demon, so there's no place for us here. We have nothing and no one."

"We've still each other." She touched his hand. "And the Mag Raith."

"You don't know what I've done." He looked away from the hurt in her eyes. "I sent the housekeeper and her behemoth of a mate back to the underworld. I collapsed a wall on the touch-reader and hers." He jabbed a claw toward Broden. "I blinded him, and his female when she healed him."

"I've no' forgotten that, you fack." The trapper's dark eyes took on a menacing glitter. "Hadnae you healed my lady, you'd be rotting now."

"You see? He knows what I am," Cul said when his sister would have spoken. "When I thought you were your mother, I intended to use you to lure Iolar here."

"Only because I made you forget me." Lilias looked down as she knotted the last strip of linen. "You repaired Mariena's skinwork."

"I caused the damage. If not for the wound I caused her, she would have come back from death on her own." That was what Lilias had intended all along, he suspected. "That was your work."

It wasn't a question, but she gave him a tiny nod.

"All right." Jenna rose to her feet to survey their work. "That should provide you with more support when you walk. Stop brow-beating your sister and try it out."

Cul met her gaze, and in it saw the same calm strength that Fiana had possessed. "Why are you doing this for me?"

"Consider it part of the peace process," Jenna said, and held out her hand. "Come on."

He allowed her to pull him up, and then tested his weight on the shattered limb. Although pain dully pulsed beneath the muscle, the wooden splints and wrappings kept his wrongly-knit bones from shifting.

He took a step before he grudgingly muttered, "It's better. Thank you."

"If the lady's willing to make peace with that half-demon," a cool voice said, "mayhap you'll do the same with yours while we check the mounts."

Lilias looked over to see Kiaran, who now stood watching them from a passage entry.

"I should speak with him," she said, though she didn't sound enthused about the prospect.

"If he gives you any grief," Jenna suggested as

she gave the falconer a narrow look, "you can always make him forget how to run his mouth."

"Aye." Lilias squared her shoulders and walked over to him.

Cul watched his sister leave the great hall with Kiaran, and only then scowled at Jenna. "If he hurts her again, I will beat him to death with your splints."

"Yeah, well, you'll probably have to stand in line." She peered up at him. "Now, how about giving me and Broden a tour of your tunnels?"

Chapter Twenty-Seven

ILIAS WALKED WITH Kiaran into the storm, where she stopped to close her eyes and turn her face up into the steady downpour. She didn't seem to care about being soaked by the rain, or concerned to be alone with him. Oddly he envied her that calm assurance. He didn't know what he would say to make amends. He'd accused her of being no better than a demon, and here she stood, paying no heed to him while bathing in a tempest.

"We should check the horses," he told her. "My brothers' mounts need be readied for battle."

She leveled a look at him, and the droplets spangling her lashes made her look as if her eyes had been bejeweled. "As you wish."

Lilias didn't say another word as she accompanied him to the stables. Once inside Kiaran checked the stalls, but found five horses already saddled. He guessed Mael or Edane had come before them, but that left him with nothing to do. As thunder shook the skies the horses shifted in their stalls, looking over the doors as if expecting to be taken out. Above them in the rafters Dive fluttered in, perching to flap the wetness from her wings.

"Do you wish to be called Treasure?" Kiaran asked.

"No." She moved away from him. "'Twas Iolar's name for me. Call me Lilias."

He connected his mind to the kestrel's. Through Dive's eyes he could see Lilias's expression as she went over to greet the mare she had been riding. The horse responded to her soft-spoken words with pleasure, but the lady looked as miserable as he felt.

He'd done that to her, reminding her of the prince. It made him wish Domnall had taken his head.

"The halfling told us how long you dwelled alone in the underworld, Lilias. I'd no notion of your loneliness." Tension made him sound harsh, so he tried to gentle his voice as he added, "I'd ask you forgive what I said in the hall."

Lilias touched her brow to the mare's head before she turned to face him. "I see. You believe my brother, your sworn enemy, but no' me, your lover. 'Tis good to ken where I stand with you."

Abruptly she moved away from the stall and headed for the doors.

"Wait." Kiaran caught her arm as she tried to pass him. He'd promised himself he wouldn't touch her again, but he couldn't seem to release her. "I've no' the chieftain's skill at peace-making. I'm truly grateful for what you did for me and my clan. 'Tis your power and secrets that trouble me."

"Dinnac forget my sire, the Sluath king," she said, her tone disinterested. "He makes me half-sister to Prince Iolar as well as Culvar."

"I've demon wings on my back, and my Viking sire enslaved and murdered my Pritani *máthair*," Kiaran reminded her. When he saw the pity in her gaze he finally let go of her. "We're the same."

"I'll never be as you." She held up her inked hand. "My skinwork, 'twill never turn to silver or gold. My flesh willnae warm, and the gold in my eyes, 'twillnae fade. I ken naught of your world."

That revelation startled him. "'Tis why you look on everything with such wonder. You've never lived as a mortal before you came to us."

"You'll find no sun-warmed strawberries in the underworld. No sound of rushing waters. No scent of flowers and herbs. No rain to feel on your skin. 'Tis all hard and cold and barren, like the Sluath." She tucked her arms around her waist. "I envy you and your clan. So much color and life and light surround you here. 'Tis marvelous, your world."

"Aye." Kiaran wished she'd think the same of him, but he'd ruined that. "'Tis much I dinnae ken of you. If you're willing to reveal more of your nature, I've questions."

"My nature as ally or enemy? A guarded secret, a prince's treasure, a demon traitor, or a heartless schemer?" Before he could reply she made a careless gesture, as if it didn't matter to her. "Choose what suits your judgment of me, Kiaran, and you'll be troubled no longer."

"My anger spoke for me in the hall." Her show of indifference didn't deceive him. He knew he'd hurt her. "I ken you're no' cruel or vicious. I dinnae believe you'd harm any of the clan. Why should you here, when you might have kept us tormented in the underworld? No, 'tis that we're much alike, and I wish to ken what *I'll* become."

Lilias's mouth tightened, but after a moment she said, "Ask your questions."

"I've wings," Kiaran said. "Will I fly as the Sluath now?"

"Aye, if there's a storm," she said. "Under clear skies you're bound to the soil."

He wondered briefly if she envied him his wings, for she had none. "You said to me three things stop the change. Love freely given, 'twas one. Tell me the others."

"'Tis what the Sluath cannae abide: courage and faith." She reached out to touch his skinwork, stopped herself, and turned away. "As long as you're brave, and loyal to your clan, you shallnae become a demon."

He wondered if it could be that simple, but the other matter remained pressing. "When I accused you of taking the memory of the day Taye died, you said 'twas my doing. What meant you by that, my lady?"

"As a lad you veiled that memory." She sighed. "'Tis what happens sometimes, when mortals endure too much suffering all at once. They lock away all remembrance, as if never 'twas. I saw it too oft among the slaves in the underworld."

"With your power, can you unlock such a memory?" When she nodded he went down on his knees before her. "Unveil the day, then. I must ken what happened after Njal killed my *máthair* and her tribe."

Lilias looked doubtful. "You dinnae fathom my meaning. Your mind sought to protect you by shrouding the day. 'Twas too much for you."

"As a lad, aye," he agreed. "I'm a man now. I survived the underworld."

"Even so, 'twas your life." Her cool hands cradled his face. "'Twillnae be pleasant, Kiaran."

"I expect naught else." He kept his gaze locked with hers. "Please, I must ken. Show me the truth."

Her hand touched his brow, and the stables became filled with branches and burning smoke.

KIARAN'S EYES stung with tears and smoke, but he waited in the bushes until Njal and his raiders finally carried off what they had looted from the burning settlement. Ash fell over him, turning his hair and tunic a whitish-gray as he retreated back into the forest. He could almost feel his mother now, her arms tugging at him as gently as the sun rose in the sky. She wished him to go back.

The weight of what he'd done suddenly became crushing. He wished he could bury Taye, but he couldn't bear to look upon her headless body. He had caused her death. He had stolen the life of the only person who loved him.

Forgive me, Máthair.

Guilt tagged after him as Kiaran walked parallel to the trail the raiders took back to their longboat. He didn't know why he followed the Vikings, but he kept enough distance between them to keep from being seen.

A terrible dread seized him as he imagined being left alone. He had no food, water or shelter. As terrible as his life had been among the Norsemen, at least he had never starved.

I should return with them.

Only when he saw the men pile onto the longboat and row away from shore did he creep out of the forest. They would hurry now, as the smoke from the burning village would be noticed by other tribes in the area. As soon as they loaded the hold they would cast off and set sail. If they left without him, Kiaran knew he would not see his sire again.

No matter what comes to pass, never go back to Noreg with them, his mother whispered inside his head.

Stranded alone in this strange land, Kiaran suspected he would die alone. It didn't frighten him now. He would give Taye justice by fulfilling her last wish.

He found an oak with low branches and climbed up as far as he could to watch the raiders. Instead of carrying their plunder down below they piled it on the deck. Quickly they began rowing out into the rough seas. An ugly storm had clouded the sky, and now stretched out over the Vikings as lightning sizzled down to pierce the seas. The dragon sail fluttered in the cold wind as the longboat moved into deeper waters, and then Kiaran noticed something odd. The sea seemed to be rising higher and higher against the hull. He recalled all the leaks down in the cargo hold.

'Tis sinking.

The Vikings became aware of their plight at the same time. The oars lifted on one side as the raiders maneuvered the longboat around and headed back toward shore. By then the swelling waves began crashing over the upper deck.

He couldn't see their faces or hear their voices, but Kiaran knew the men would be in a panic now. They'd gone too far out to swim to shore. The icy waters would kill them in minutes. Their ship tossed up and down before the bow steadily rose into the air. The stern went under the sea as the Vikings began jumping into the dark waves. Like a water bird the longboat sank down and disappeared. The heads of the raiders bobbed for a few more moments before they, too, were swallowed up.

Wiped away clean, as if they had never come here, had never existed.

Kiaran sat for a long time in the oak as he watched the dark, roiling sea. He felt much like those waters, lifeless and empty. Everything he had been, all the wrongs he had done, would never be known. Nor would the Pritani or Norse ever ken what had become of Taye and her tribe, or Njal and his raiders. Kiaran's world had been scoured clean of all but him by the hand of the Gods.

At sunset he climbed down from the oak and found his way into a meadow filled with flowers.

There he staggered and fell, wailing as he wept for all that he had lost, and would never have again.

Lilias saw every moment of Kiaran's past as he faced it, and throbbed with the echoes of the terrible horror he had felt that day. Losing his mother had inflicted on him a crushing, grinding guilt that he still carried. Yet watching the Viking longboat sink had caused the boy he had been to create the veil. For some reason he had not wished to recall his sire's grim fate. When he came out of the remembrance, he looked at her with the same stunned confusion Culvar had shown when she'd restored his memories.

"'Twillnae hurt you, the past," Lilias told him gently. "As you said, you're no' that lad anymore. To ken, 'twill but set right what remains amiss in you."

Slowly Kiaran stood, and his face lost all expression. "Had they no' fled what they'd done, they'd have taken the plunder below, and found the leaks had grown far worse. They'd never have set sail with a flooded hold. Instead they paid for that raid with their lives."

He'd believed all this time that his sire had escaped back to his homeland. Now Lilias understood.

"You wished to suffer, to punish yourself for Taye's death." As grief for him beset her, she drew her hands from his face. "Remembering that Njal and his raiders drowned stood in the way of that."

"Aye." He let out his breath, and his eyes darkened. "'Twould seem that the Gods took twice their vengeance."

"I dinnae ken your gods, but should they avenge themselves on the young for being left stranded and alone…ah." New sorrow flooded through her, and she took a shaky breath. "Mayhap 'tis why they sent you to me. You're my punishment."

"Never." Kiaran gathered her close, his hands spreading over her back to caress her gently. "'Twas chance that brought us together, but your kind heart that drew me to you."

"I feel it beating in my breast, but 'tisnae mortal or demon," she whispered to him. "Mayhap my very being offends your Gods."

"No, my lady, no." He kissed the top of her head. "You couldnae help being born to a brute and a slave any more than I."

Lilias encircled his waist with her arms, and felt his body reacting and changing to her closeness. His muscles went taut, his shaft swelled, and the scent of him grew hot and intoxicating. Yet he made no move to do more than comfort her, as if that were all that mattered to him.

Still he did not know everything about her, and Lilias knew the time had come to reveal the last.

"When night falls," she told him, drawing back and taking hold of his hands, "Iolar and the horde shall come. He favors using darkness to hide their approach when they cull groups of mortals. I must show you something more. Come."

She led him up to the loft, where she opened the shutters.

Kiaran joined her, and looked out at the trees being threshed by the driving winds and lashing rain. "I see the storm ravaging the forest, but no Sluath."

"I've one last secret to unveil." Lilias had lived cloaked in illusion for so long that she felt naked as she dropped her glamour. "'Tis me."

Chapter Twenty-Eight

AFTER DISCUSSING HOW they would change their plans, Mariena left Domnall working in the forge, but nearly collided with Broden outside in the passage. Her man looked furious, and when he pulled her into his arms he held her so tightly she felt her ribs groan.

"I love you to embrace me, *mon charmant*," she said carefully, "but please to remember you may snap me like the twig." She dragged in some air. "Any moment, in fact."

"Forgive me." Broden eased his grip and buried his face in her pale hair. His hard chest moved against her breasts as he used the slow, steady technique she had taught him. Focusing on his breathing helped him control the temper that he never dared lose.

Something very serious had angered him. Since they'd mated he hadn't once slipped into a rage.

"What has happened?" she asked, slipping her hand up to stroke his neck. "You perhaps killed the monster while I was gone?"

"No one has died. Yet." He sighed, and some of the tension left his body. "'Tis naught."

She had sensed the worry and anger that had been building in him since the day Lilias had arrived at Dun Chaill. With Broden's superhuman strength, however, he couldn't allow himself to explode.

"You must tell me this naught, *mon couer*," she told him firmly. "Or I will lock you in the mill house to crush more stone until you feel better."

"Too oft I think on the day you took my death from me, and I awoke to find you…" He stopped and shook his head. "Soon we shall face death again. If we dinnae prevail over the Sluath, 'twill be no coming back for either of us."

She took hold of his hot face and made him look into her eyes. "Then we die, my brave and too-handsome husband, as we live now. Together, in love." She smiled. "Only I think for this death I would like you to be on top of me."

His beautiful eyes gleamed as he bent his head, and brushed an achingly soft kiss over her lips before he murmured against her ear, "I'd be inside you right now, *ma belle*."

A thrilling shiver ran through Mariena. It always drove her mad when he spoke in the French she was teaching him.

"That must wait for later," she said as she drew back. "What made you think of that terrible day?"

"That facking Culvar." He dragged a hand over the back of his neck. "He's burrowed so many tunnels under Dun Chaill 'tis a miracle the castle doesnae collapse. 'Twas how he vanished so quickly after he repaired your skinwork. He's kept them concealed with illusions. Each time we might have found a passage or entry, we saw but earth or solid stone."

Although she understood why that had enraged her man, Mariena felt a very reluctant surge of admiration for their half-demon host. "And the gate?"

He nodded. "'Tis there, just as 'twas the night

we first came. He keeps it guarded. He's an army of iron warriors below."

"He controls these things still, no? And they are made of the only metal that kills the Sluath." When he nodded she kissed his cheek. "So, we must keep this peace with Culvar."

"Then dinnae leave me alone with him," Broden muttered.

After giving him a second, longer kiss on the mouth Mariena sent him into the forge so he could report what he had found to Domnall. She returned to the great hall, where she spied Jenna and Mael with Ewan, but no sign of Lilias's brother.

"Where is Culvar?" she asked the chieftain's wife.

Jenna pointed to the floor. "He's looking through a bunch of old scrolls he had squirreled away down there. Apparently he left some traps off the map we found." She saw Mariena's expression and lifted her hands. "I'm sorry, but not like he can hide from us anymore. We know where he lives now."

"Pah. You think you may find him in these many tunnels that go to where we do not know?

And drag him from them?" Mariena waved a hand. "Never mind. I will go."

"A wee offering of trust, lass, 'tis oft swaying," Ewan called to them from his seat by the hearth. "The great beast, I reckon he's no different than any proud warrior. Aside from the claws and teeth and demon's eyes, ye ken. Leave him, and he shall return."

She went over to crouch down before him. "You were mortal when you came here, no?" When he nodded she sat back on her heels. "How did you convince Culvar not to kill you, *Monsieur*?"

The old man sighed. "I gave him my word I'd never speak of our pact. Should I, the beast shallnae keep his vow to me, but he shall cut off my head. I favor where 'tis."

"Egad, we cannot have any more threats of beheadings. They make me quite nervous." Rosealise appeared with a bowl of steaming pottage, which she carefully placed in the old Pritani's hands. "Do keep your word to Culvar, my dear sir."

Ewan peered up at her. "Ye're a lovely, strapping thing. Ye're sure ye're no' Mag Raith?"

"I'm of an English clan, I'm afraid." Rosealise

retrieved a small table and placed it by his chair. "Ah, the Britanni people, I believe you call them."

"Ah, so ye're from the far south, then." The shaman nodded. "I'd have reckoned ye Viking with that sunny hair, only ye're too kindly. Many of their larger females take up the blade as if born to make war. I recall one spring, or mayhap 'twas summer…"

Leaving the old man to charm the housekeeper, Mariena went to join Mael and Jenna. "Very well. We will leave Culvar to his scroll searching for now. We must change some of the passage diversions. Domnall wishes to channel the demons into the tunnels below rather than into his traps."

The chieftain's wife frowned. "But if we do that, they'll find the open gate to the underworld. They'll escape."

"Exactly." Mariena tucked her arm through Jenna's. "Now come with me, and I'll tell you why we wish them to."

Chapter Twenty-Nine

A CURTAIN OF white and scarlet light engulfed Lilias, and poured like liquid fire over her form as Kiaran stared. Whatever was happening to her seemed to be stripping away every part of her being. Her borrowed garments slid down from her limbs and torso, falling to her feet like a skin she had discarded. The air between them crackled with the power pouring from her glowing hands and swirling around her.

Did she meant to end herself?

"No." Kiaran rushed to her, and yet the moment he took hold of her the enchantment ended. He found himself holding another woman entirely.

"Dinnae be alarmed," she said in a voice like singing water. "'Tis me."

"By the Gods," he murmured, entranced, unable to move.

Hair streaked with the colors of flame and snow spilled over her shoulders to fall down around her slim hips. All of her flesh had gone rosy-white, and shone as if polished from within. From her back arched graceful wings of garnet-banded white. Short golden claws tipped the long fingers of her slim hands.

"I meant to show you, that first night in your tower," she said. "Only I couldnae find the courage."

The luminous perfection of her features could be compared to nothing of his understanding. She no longer resembled Lilias or any mortal female he'd seen. To look upon her loveliness humbled and lifted him, all at once. Her large, slanted eyes, now a sparkling gold with streaks of emerald and blue, invoked lush glens, peaceful lochs, and sun-drenched skies. Her exquisite face possessed such radiance that he wanted to fall to his knees in worship.

Yet for all her unearthly splendor she showed the flush of mortal blood beneath her immaculate skin, and the warmth of emotion in her smile. As his shock faded he noticed the faintest resemblance to the Lilias she had been in the curve of her ears and brows, and the graceful lines of her throat. Everything about her drew Kiaran. Even her hair radiated a tranquilly sweet scent, like that of dew-spangled lilies.

She hadn't become a demon, or a mortal, but some astounding fusion of both.

Stepping back, she made a slow turn so that he saw every inch of her magnificent form. Facing him, she folded back her wings and made a gesture with her marked hand, and a new band of magic wrapped around her. The shimmer became a simple shift of white and gold that covered her nakedness.

Kiaran suspected this was the reason she had always seemed so perfect. Magic had created Lilias. The real female beneath the illusion had been sired by the Sluath king, whom she obviously favored. From what she had just demonstrated she also possessed far more power than he'd ever imagined.

"Why didnae you show yourself to me thus?" Before she could answer he recalled how she had appeared in the tunnels the night they'd met, and made the final connection. "You used illusion to hide yourself *before* we came into the underworld."

She nodded. "Culvar saw to it that I kept my true form cloaked in my mortal *máthair's* image. He wouldnae allow me leave the chamber as myself. He reckoned if the guards caught me, they'd believe me Fiana."

Her mother's name gave him pause. Galan Aedth had once been mated to a Pritani female by the same name, but Kiaran recalled Edane saying that she had died giving birth in the druid's first incarnation. "She's a lovely lady."

"I ever wished I had her beauty, so 'twas never a hardship to disguise myself as her." Sorrow painted itself on her exquisite face. "Later, wearing her image became a comfort of sorts. I'd but to look in a mirror to see her."

Since Fiana had been mortal, Kiaran suspected she wouldn't have survived as long as her daughter in the underworld. "When did she die?"

"Soon after Culvar escaped." She glanced down at herself, grimacing as if what she saw displeased her. "I ken that I'm as fearful to behold as the Sluath. 'Twas why I kept myself cloaked before you and the clan here. I wished you to befriend me first before I revealed all."

"I'm no' afraid of you, my lady. Never could one so lovely and alive be a demon." He lifted his hand to her face, and stroked his fingertips along the splendor of her cheek. "Aye, 'tis fitting for Domnall to call you 'Princess.'"

"I reckoned you'd be angered." She looked uncertain now. "What you said in the hall, 'twas truth. In this I've deceived you and your clan from the beginning."

"As I've done in my way. Again, we're the same." He wanted to trace the sensual bow of her bottom lip, to discover if it felt as soft as it had each time he'd kissed her. "What name shall I call you now, my lady?"

"I've truly none," she admitted. "Fiana wouldnae name me, nor allow Culvar to call me anything but sister or child." She rubbed her cheek against his hand. "I want the name you gave me."

"Lilias, then. I'll take you back to the stronghold." And he would, Kiaran decided, as soon as he made himself stop touching her.

His fingers rebelled, sliding under the frost-fire of her hair to feel the luxurious weight of her tresses. She had the very softest mane, as light and downy as fluff on a new chick. He wanted to feel the glorious silk of it caressing the sides of his face, the vault of his chest, the iron-hard muscles of his thighs.

"I must show myself to the clan, then." She shifted closer, as if to take comfort from the press of his body against hers. "Will you stay with me? I dinnae feel so fearful when you're near."

The sound of hard rain pelting the roof over their heads matched the rapid beat of her heart against his. As the wind flung more drops through the window to spatter them, the cool scent of her altered, becoming like moonlight on the wind. Kiaran felt his own wings arch from his spine, every feather making itself felt with a curious heated ache.

"What do you to me?" he murmured against her brow.

"The storm," she whispered. "'Tis stirring our senses."

Nightfall would not arrive for hours. He had finished his work in the forge. He knew the clan had done the same with their preparations in the stronghold. This might be the last moment he could share alone with Lilias before the battle.

Kiaran folded his wings around her, wrapping her in his fiery feathers as he brought his mouth to hers. Against her lips he said, "Then let us wake them."

※

BEING ENFOLDED by the silken feathers of Kiaran's wings made Lilias tremble with delight, but it was the hunger of his mouth on hers that ignited a deep, fiery throb between her thighs. That he kissed her while she remained in her true form made wild excitement rise inside her, growing and distending like the thick shaft she felt against her belly now.

She didn't repel him. He wanted her as she was.

He lifted his head so that his breath whispered across her damp, swollen lips.

"'Tisnae to stop the change, or for comfort, or to forget the past. Give me your passion, my lady, and you shall have the measure of mine, as should ever be between us."

Lilias had never touched him without her cloak of glamour between them. Until this moment she'd never realized how the magic had muted her senses. Everything he was flooded into her, perhaps heightened by the intensity of the gathering storm. The heavy throb of his heart pounded under her palm and echoed in her bones. The airy coolness of his scent filled her head like a moonlit breeze running through her blood. He must have felt the same, for he murmured that she tasted of sunlight.

"You're my passion, my love," she whispered.

His hands came around her hips, and slid down the curve of her spine until he gripped her bottom. Lifting her up, he carried her to the window, where he stepped onto the sill. She gripped the sides of the frame as he tore loose the laces of his trews and then pushed up the edge of her shift. Rain lashed her wings and his face, but when she looked into his eyes she saw herself reflected. She had become as tiny stars in his twilight gaze.

"Kiaran." With the wind at her back she wanted him to embrace what they were. "Take me into the storm."

He muttered under his breath, shaking against her as he took hold of his shaft with his fist and pressed between her thighs. The moment his cockhead touched her quim she gushed for him, her folds blooming as he pushed between and entered her softness. Once he had seated his tip inside her, he took hold of her legs and pulled them up around his waist.

His magnificent wings flared out, and then he leapt into the wind, soaring up with her into the sky.

They'd shared love-making many times, and yet as they flew nothing of it felt familiar. He made love to her, the real Lilias, in the midst of a storm funneling all its power into them. Lilias held him tightly as he came deeper into her, and felt the delicious stretch of her body as she accepted his thick girth inside herself. The wind buffeted them as he took them higher, their bodies becoming saturated with rain.

His kestrels appeared, and spiraled around them as if celebrating their joining.

Making love with Kiaran had been the most mortal thing Lilias had ever experienced, and yet in the sky it became some inexplicable tangle that she would never unravel. They became creatures of air and fire, two things she had never truly been. As if her body knew her thoughts, a strange heat ignited where they had joined, and flashed up into her belly. It spread, consuming everything dull and cold that remained within from the underworld.

"How can we burn so?" she called to him over the rush of the wind.

"Your pretty quim sets fire to me," Kiaran said, growling the words as he spun with her to hover far above the stronghold. "Now I shall stoke yours with my cock."

She shook as he plowed deep, skewering her until she felt the thick base of his root against her opening. Then he took her mouth with his, ravishing her with his tongue while his shaft pumped in and out of her. All the while he rode the winds and rain with her, their bodies entwined. Her sweet, aching need abruptly billowed into wrenching, demanding desire. For all the delirious sensations he gave her she wanted more. He worked himself over a place inside her that tightened and swelled and then made her clench on him with feverish, quaking desperation.

Lilias heard herself wailing inside her head, and whimpering from her lips.

"Naught could take you from me entire," he told her, and brought his hand to her swelling breast. "Since my return no other could satisfy me. Now I ken why. You took my memories, but my body never forgot yours."

His stroking thumb against her nipple made her writhe on the driving power of his cock.

"You never left me, *m'anam*," Lilias said, moaning the words. "I kept you in my thoughts. I came to you in my dreams. Ever I woke with the taste of you on my lips."

The thrust of his shaft into her grew harder and faster as he gripped her mound and put his mouth to her ear. As he took her higher and higher, he told her of all the nights he'd lain alone in his bed, stroking his cock as he wished for a woman he'd never and always known. He'd spilled himself again and again for her without even a memory of her face.

"Now I shall fill you to the brim with my loving," Kiaran murmured. "My seed shall spill down your thighs like the rain. The clan shall smell me on you and ken you're mine."

Lilias cried out as a tempest of wanton bliss engulfed her, and flung her arms around him as she felt him stiffen in reaction to her peak. He thrust one final time, and his cock jerked inside her. He groaned as he pumped his seed deep into her core, plummeting toward the earth before he caught the air with his wings. The heat of his silken fluids bathed her clenching quim with so much heat she thought flames from their joining would devour them both.

Somehow he brought them back down to the stables to land on the window ledge. His arms trembled as he climbed down, still inside her, holding her firmly against him. He carried her over to a loose mound of golden hay. There he lowered himself, keeping their sexes joined, and rolled onto his back to lay with her atop him.

The dry, sunny scent of the straw rose around them as Lilias collapsed onto his chest. The earthiness of the stable pleased her as much as his shaft nestled inside her body. Nothing made her feel more human than this, even with their wings spread out on either side of them. She wanted to tell him all of this, but she couldn't bring herself to move or speak yet. She never wished to again if it meant separating herself from Kiaran.

Sometime later he stroked his hand over her back. "When 'tis done, the battle with the Sluath, we should declare ourselves before the clan, and become mates."

"I think we should return to this loft and make our home here." Lilias lifted her head to regard him. Judging by his expression he wasn't making a jest. "Truly? You'd want me as wife? A barren halfling?"

He brought her inked hand to his mouth and kissed her fingertips. "If you'll have me as husband, aye. We've both wings. I cannae sire a bairn. We're immortal. 'Tis the perfect match, I reckon."

After being loved by him in the storm Lilias would have happily vowed to give him whatever pleased him. Yet he had not spoken of his feelings for her, only his desire. She also wondered if he had thought through what might become of them once they announced their bond to the others.

"Your clan may oppose this 'perfect match.'" She propped herself up on one elbow. "Indeed, once I reveal myself to them, they may bid me leave Dun Chaill."

Kiaran caressed her cheek. "Then I shall follow my heart and go with you. Be my lady wife, Lilias."

He hadn't said he loved her, but that was close enough. He also didn't seem too terribly concerned by the prospect of abandoning the clan. Lilias knew only that it would be very different when they faced the others, and she would not force him to choose between her and the Mag Raith.

"Ask me again on the morrow," she said finally, and laughed as he rolled over and showered her with hay as he tucked her under his big body. "Kiaran. We should join the others in the stronghold."

"We shall." He kissed each corner of her mouth. "Before nightfall."

Chapter Thirty

※◆※

ROSEALISE REFUSED TO be useless as the rest of the clan finished their preparations, and spent the afternoon at her work table stuffing small, loose bundles of linen with sand and thorns. The chieftain had asked her to make more, as her mixture had proven quite useful during their last battle with the Sluath. Tossing a bundle into a demon's face would cause the sand and thorns to burst out, temporarily but effectively blinding it. Even with her laughable lack of skill with a crossbow, a well placed bundle might give even her enough time to shoot one of the demons.

She had never thought herself capable of killing any living creature, but now that Lilias had restored her memories of the underworld, she had no qualms.

As Rosealise worked she also prepared a large kettle of soothing brew no one had time to drink, and baked some rounds of oat bread to go with a roasting chicken the clan would likely be too busy to eat. She consoled herself with the notion that after the battle the clan would likely be hungry.

The act of cooking also comforted her. Nothing seemed more life-affirming than the preparation of food, especially in the dreary, dragging hours before a battle.

At first Mael looked in on her whenever he passed near the kitchens, nodding his approval at her mound of bundles. He and Nellie then left the stronghold to herd the sheep and cattle into pastures farthest away from the castle. Rosealise felt touched by their concern for the safety of their animals, for the Sluath would not hesitate to harm or kill them if they strayed into the field of battle.

Toward the end of the afternoon her husband returned, his big frame taut, and surprised her by sitting down beside her.

Rosealise set aside the last bundle she'd tied. "All is well, I hope?"

"At dusk Jenna and Domnall shall accompany some of the iron warriors to patrol the battlements and keep watch," he told her. "I'm for the tower watch. Edane took Ewan and Culvar to the barrier to fathom if they may strengthen the spell, and set some traps there. Mariena and Broden work below to block all tunnels but that which leads to the underworld gate. When Culvar returns, I need convince him of Domnall's scheme."

His deep voice sounded calm, but Rosealise could see the trepidation in his topaz eyes.

"Lilias and Kiaran have not yet emerged from the stables," she told him as she poured him a mug of her soothing brew. "I daresay they shall, once they've settled matters between them. Perhaps the lady will convince her brother to go along with the chieftain's plan."

"If such even matters," Mael said with a sigh. "With that leg Culvar maynae fight. That leaves eleven of us."

"We have many more iron warriors, and Dun Chaill to protect us." She covered his hand with hers. "You've done all you can do, my dear. The rest is up to God, or the Gods, as you'd have it."

"Mayhap we die this night, or tomorrow we

live." He gave her a sideways look. "To ken you've a tomorrow, my lady, I'd give back my immortality and my power. Aye, and my life."

"Nonsense." Rosealise twined her fingers with his. "I would never have such bad manners as to outlive you, my dear sir. Well, perhaps for a day so that I might give you a proper burial, but then I should die of a broken heart atop your grave. Everyone knows that is the very worst of deaths. Perhaps that is why it always happens in novels. Nevertheless, I utterly refuse to muddle on alone, my dearest one. Without you, I have no tomorrow."

Mael tugged her into his arms, placing her like a child on his lap and tucking her head under his chin.

"'Tisnae possible for me to love you more, I ever reckon," he told her, stroking the curls that had come loose around her nape. "And then you speak from the heart, and I find I do."

They sat together in that comforting fashion for a time until Rosealise heard splashing steps outside the kitchens, and reluctantly extracted herself from her husband's arms. She smiled when she saw Kiaran enter, and then saw what came up behind him and nearly fainted.

Mael knocked aside the work table as he sprang to his feet, sending his mug toppling. "Behind you." As brew splashed to the floor, he drew his sword and put himself between her, the falconer and the demon that had followed him.

"No, Brother," Kiaran countered, holding up his hands. "Stop. 'Tisnae what you think."

"'Tis a facking demon," the seneschal shouted, brandishing his blade.

A shower of red and white light wrapped around the Sluath, and a moment later it transformed into Lilias.

"By the Gods." Mael's sword arm came down as quickly as his jaw. "'Tis the lass."

"Forgive me, I didnae intend to startle you." The Pritani woman gave the falconer a narrow look. "I told you I should wear my cloak."

Peering around her husband's arm, Rosealise then cautiously stepped out. "You've been wearing rather more than a cloak, I should think."

"'Tis my true form," Lilias quickly said and explained how she had been using a body ward to appear like her mortal mother. "I wish to show myself to the rest of the clan as soon as I may."

"Perhaps you should remain in *this* guise, and

warn them before removing it," Rosealise suggested drily.

Hitching, thumping footsteps approached the entry from the great hall, and a very wet and bedraggled Culvar limped inside. He regarded his sister and the falconer for a long moment, his distorted mouth curling into a sneer before he turned to the seneschal. "We've done what we can with the barrier."

"'Tis more we'd ask of you. We wish to send the Sluath through your open gate, and then have you seal it as you've done with the others." Mael glanced at Lilias. "Domnall asked if you'd explain the rest to him."

She nodded.

Rosealise brought more mugs to the table and began filling them. To Culvar she said, "Please, sir, do sit down and rest your leg while you talk, and mind the spill there." Once he did she handed him a mug and carried the rest out on a tray into the hall.

Edane stood with Ewan by the hearth, their sodden clothes dripping into a growing puddle around their boots. The archer looked grim, but the old shaman seemed none the worse for his soaking.

As she walked toward them Rosealise felt something prickling beneath her skirt, and realized it came from her Sluath tattoo. She also knew inexplicably that Meirneal had caused the sensation.

"The barrier, 'tis stronger, but 'twillnae hold back the Sluath for long," Edane told her. "And now sunset is upon us."

Rosealise hurried outside, where she turned to look all around until she saw glowing, swelling lights in the sky to the west. She looked up at the battlements as she brought her reed whistle to her lips to blow two long, high notes.

Chapter Thirty-One

FLYING THROUGH THE tempest-filled skies at the front of Iolar and the Sluath deeply gratified Galan. Never had he felt more sure of himself or his future. Although he had suffered near-ceaseless agony to attain it, he had at last taken his proper place as their leader. Once they vanquished the Mag Raith he would be crowned as their king.

The weight of his new position didn't trouble him in the slightest. He had the knowledge from dozens of lifetimes, his druid training, and his Sluath power. He alone could rule both the demons in the underworld, and the humans in the mortal realm. In time, he suspected, his dominion would grow until he became known among all of his subjects as their god. Indeed, after this battle, he would see to it that every living creature in both worlds worshipped him thus.

He deserved nothing less than fearful, slavish adoration.

The nettling rain slapped his face as he soared ever higher, aware that the demons following him struggled to keep pace. They had grown soft and weak, languishing here in the mortal realm. That he would never permit again.

"Where are you taking us?" a snide voice called. "London?"

He glanced down to spy Iolar's haughty glower as the prince flew alongside Danar.

"'Tisnae far now." Galan imagined commanding the big demon to pin down the petulant weakling as he slowly sawed off his pretty head.

The two Sluath stupidly believed they had fooled him again with their fawning and false promises. Once he used them to defeat the Pritani, Galan would slaughter them both—and take his time with Iolar. After that, the rest of the demons would be easily controlled. Seeing him end their two strongest would keep them fearful and obsequious.

Then he would turn his attention to lovely, lying, whoring Fiana.

Lightning danced through the night sky as they passed over the burnt smear left of Wachvale. He turned to guide the demons to the spot where he had twice breeched the spell barrier. As he drew near he felt new power radiating from the magic boundary. Breathing in, he caught the now-familiar stink of old Pritani spellwork.

Culvar had at last allied himself with the Mag Raith. Galan would see to it that he lived long enough to regret that grave mistake. Stopping to hover in front of the barrier, he summoned his own magic.

"What are you doing?" Iolar demanded. "There's nothing here but an old forest."

"I don't see any castle or rebels," Meirneal whined as he flapped alongside Galan. "Have you perhaps lost your way, tree-lick…ah, my king?"

Galan swatted him aside before he held out his hands and unleashed his power. It slammed into the barrier, crackling over it like a burst of dark lightning.

Danar hovered at a safer distance as he took in the huge wall, now made visible to the demons.

"Whoever cast this spell has considerable

power, my liege." He tossed one of his blades at the barrier, and then reflexively caught it when it bounced back at him. "And impressive cunning. Nothing will pass through it now."

"They seek to keep my mortal spies from attacking," he told the big demon. "They dinnae ken I lead you to Dun Chaill."

Arcs of Galan's magic wormed across the shimmering wall, wriggling like hungry serpents as they searched for and found small patches of weakness. There they began to eat away at the spell.

"This is taking forever," Clamhan said as he swooped down. His skull mask emitted a sharp crack as he tried to ram himself through one of the holes. The barrier exploded with magic, hurling him into the trees where he became impaled on a thick branch and screeched.

Galan chuckled as he watched the demon writhe like a pierced insect.

"We will need him if we're to prevail, my liege," Danar said.

Annoyed now, Galan flicked his finger to send a cutting swath of magic that sheared the branch from the tree. Clamhan plummeted to the ground, where his mask shattered and pelted the mud. As Seabhag dropped down to jerk out the branch, Meirneal darted through another hole, landed on the other side, and turned with a gloating expression.

"Ha. You're too big–"

A gush of black blood cut off the small demon's voice as he looked down at the iron blade that had emerged from his belly.

Behind him an iron warrior rose from a mound of leaves. The enchanted statue kicked Meirneal's legs out from under him and wrenched its sword free. The little cannibal turned his head to look at Galan, his eyes wide as he gurgled a wordless plea.

"Do something," Iolar hissed at him.

"Why?" Galan countered. "He's already dead."

As if it had heard him the warrior silently swung its blade down, and neatly decapitated Meirneal.

As the other demons screamed with rage, Galan watched Meirneal's body shrivel into a tiny twisted ball of rotted flesh. He noticed other mounds and piles of detritus that extended along the inside of the barrier. All appeared large enough to camouflage more iron warriors, which provided an unhappy revelation.

The Mag Raith not only knew about the Sluath attack, they had prepared for it.

"We stay in the air until we reach the castle," he told the rest of the horde, and then summoned more power as he turned his attention to the barrier.

Chapter Thirty-Two

AS SOON AS he heard Rosealise's warning, Kiaran interrupted his lady. "We've no more time for talk. They've come."

Lilias rose and touched Culvar's shoulder. "I ken you desire their deaths, but what the chieftain has planned, 'twill be a far worse fate. You'll secure Dun Chaill and the mortal realm for all time. Please, say you shall leave the gate open."

The halfling looked up at his sister for a long moment before he nodded. Pain flickered across his face as she embraced him, but Kiaran saw something more in the demon's eyes: love. Then Culvar got to his feet and hobbled out into the hall.

"I must speak to the chieftain for a moment," Lilias told him.

"They'll be at the stables by now." Kiaran took her hand before they rushed out into the storm.

Summoning all his kestrels, Kiaran used their eyes to scan every horizon, and saw the glittering light to the west. Bursts of magic fountained high into the air as the spell barrier appeared and then seemed to thin. When they entered the stables, he saw the other four Mag Raith leading their mounts from their stalls.

"They're nearly through the boundary," Kiaran told Domnall. "Culvar has agreed to keep the gate open. Lilias and I shall take to the sky with the kestrels, and lead the demons to you. Once they're close enough, you may lure them into the stronghold."

"Lilias?" Broden said, frowning. "She cannae fly."

"In truth," she said, dropping her cloak and spreading her wings, "I can." She turned to Domnall, who looked just as stunned as the trapper. "As your lady would say, 'tis a long story, and we've no time." She dropped down on one knee and bowed her head. "I pledge my loyalty to you and the Mag Raith, Chieftain. I shallnae betray you."

Domnall helped her to her feet. "Never I reckoned you would, Princess." He drew his dagger, and offered her the hilt. "You'll need a weapon."

"Forgive me, but I cannae," she told him, taking a step back. "Iron, 'tis deadly to me."

Thinking of how he'd left her surrounded by iron in the aviary made Kiaran feel sick. "But you've the skinwork, and immortality. Surely they protect you."

"In some ways I'm just as any Sluath." Lilias touched her marked hand. "Thanks to my sire my memory power came at birth, and immortality over time, no' from my skinwork."

"By the Gods. The carved shell pendant you wore, 'twas hers?" As she nodded Domnall looked thunderstruck. He started to say something, and then shook his head. "We shall speak of her later, Princess."

Edane shouldered his bow. "You must take shelter in the shielded blind with our ladies, Lilias. You cannae face the demons unarmed." His eyes widened as she summoned her power, which made her entire body glow. "Or no'."

"Dinnae fear," she told him as she spread her wings. "My magic, 'tis nearly as powerful as Iolar's." She closed her eyes for a moment. "I can feel them approaching. We must go now."

Kiaran looked at each man, and felt his heart swelling with emotion. He might lose one or more of them today, or die himself, but he would always be their brother. He wanted them to remember that.

He thrust out his fist. "Mag Raith *gu bràth*."

Three more fists touched his before Domnall covered them with his big hand, and they all repeated the oath that had bonded them as brothers. "Mag Raith *gu bràth*."

Kiaran turned to his lady and held out his hand.

Lilias hurried out of the stables with him, her hand tightly clasping his. The kestrels came from all directions to hover above them, each raptor uttering a short, sharp cry. As he and his lady spread their wings, Kiaran opened his mind fully to the flight to share their senses. They soared up together to join the kestrels on the tearing winds and flew west.

As they passed over the castle Kiaran glanced

down to see iron warriors armed with bows positioned along the walls of the battlements and at the window slits in the standing towers. A tiny flutter of white from a window slit in the rebuilt tower, the signal Jenna had promised, assured him that the ladies had retreated to their warded blind there. He felt a jolt as a thin white bolt sizzled between him and Lilias, and scattered his kestrels into a wider circle as he glided over her.

Before them stretched a wall of dark blue light that had begun to crumble in on itself. Beyond it Kiaran could see the malevolent glow of the Sluath behind a large, dark silhouette of black and silver, and then another flashing bolt illuminated the huge demon's features.

Casting streams of power from his clawed hands, Galan Aedth struck the barrier again and again. When he saw them, his eyes took on an eerie yellow glow, and he gathered a huge sphere of dark light, hurling it at the boundary. It collapsed in the next moment.

"Now," Prince Iolar shouted.

Kiaran changed direction, diving down in front of Lilias to protect her as the Sluath came racing toward them. He saw a few dozen following Galan and the prince, and none coming behind those. Nearly all of the horde looked ragged and ashen. Many had blackened garments hanging from burned flesh.

"Mag Raith," the druid bellowed as he flew straight for them.

"Turn back," Kiaran shouted to her over his shoulder just as curtains of lightning streaked down around them.

Lilias nimbly dodged the bolts, but one glanced off his right wing. The strike burned through his feathers to send crippling, fiery pain stabbing into his back. Desperately Kiaran tried to stay aloft, and then Lilias seized him and carried him to the ground. There she landed, dragging him into some brush. She cradled him against her as she squinted against the pouring rain to scan the skies above the castle.

"We shall hide here, and Domnall and the others shall come," she told him, and then folded her wings around him as the demons began to descend. "Dinnae try to fly again. Your wing, 'tis broken."

Kiaran knew in that moment what he had to do. "Stay here," he told her gently. "I'll see to them."

Lilias shook her head. "No, you cannae, they're too many. I love you. I shallnae—"

"You shall." He caught her up against him and kissed her with all the affection he would never again lavish on her. "You'll never lose me, for I'm in your heart. I love you, Wife."

Her magic swirled around them, and when it shimmered away he looked into the flawless face of his Pritani lass.

"The prince shallnae harm his Treasure," she told him, and then bolted from the brush out into the pasture.

Clawed hands seized her as soon as she stepped into sight, and Lilias did not resist. Kiaran's rage swelled as she was tossed to the sodden ground in front of Galan and Iolar.

"My treasure," the prince crooned, reaching for her, only to be knocked aside by the druid.

"No one touches her," Galan said as he cast a stream of power over their heads, forming a shield against the torrents of rain. He crouched down to peer into Lilias's face, and in a very different voice he said, "Fiana, my love. You've come back to me at last." His lips stretched into a ghastly grin. "How terrible for you."

Kiaran surged forward to burst from the

brush and confront the druid, only to be yanked backward as a huge clawed hand clamped over his mouth.

"No' a sound," Culvar murmured before he dragged him down into darkness.

Chapter Thirty-Three

RAIN AND SLEET dripped from the faces of the demons leering at Lilias, but only Iolar and the strange black and silver demon possessed the full beauty of the Sluath. Something terrible had happened to the rest of the horde. The others seemed to be withering in on themselves, their pallid flesh as dull as their sunken eyes. Most had been burned, and still carried horrific wounds. Even Danar, the strongest of Iolar's lackies, stood to one side, half his face blackened, his wide shoulders slumped.

But the strange demon Lilias recognized. He'd been the one with the bow who had meant to kill Kiaran, that day when her mare had flung her into the maze.

"Galan," the prince said to the dark demon with exaggerated patience. "You're mistaken. Your wife died long ago. This slave is mine. She's always been mine." He glanced down at her with greed in his eyes. "My very own special treasure."

Lilias thought quickly. The new demon had to be Galan Aedth, the druid headman of the tribe that the Mag Raith had protected for so many centuries. But how had he been transformed, and why would he call her by her *máthair's* name when they had never met?

"You think I dinnae ken my mate?" Galan shouted at the prince as he took hold of Lilias by the throat and jerked her from the ground. "I watched her die birthing my wretch of a son in my first life. Only 'twas a ruse so she might run off with her lovers, and leave me to tend to her brat. Then you facks took her when you captured the Mag Raith."

Danar stepped forward. "You're mistaken, my liege. This female was culled, ah, in the last century." His brows drew together. "I believe. I cannot quite recall when."

"We never culled the Mag Raith," Clamhan added. "They came to us. And if you keep that up, Druid, you're going to snap her neck."

Lilias pretended to struggle against Galan's grip as if he had cut off her air and was crushing her throat. When he dropped her, she looked up at him feigning dread and terror, as if a helpless mortal.

"I'm no' your Fiana," she told him, gasping the words, "but I ken what happened to her. She belonged to the Sluath king." She waited a moment before she added, "My sire."

"What?" Iolar laughed heartily. "Now the little slut claims to be my sister. Really, is there anyone you're not, Treasure?"

Ignoring him, Lilias slowly got to her feet, pushing her wet hair back from her face.

"The king wished to breed with mortal females," she said to Galan, "so he sent the horde to collect those proven fertile. He also desired to torment them, as it added to his pleasure, and so he demanded females who had died in childbirth."

Danar stiffened, and his muddy eyes narrowed. "My liege, this female is obviously demented. Let me end her madness."

"A demon cannot breed with a dead human," Galan told her flatly.

"Unless the king's halfling son first resurrected

them," she said. As the demons began muttering, Lilias clasped her hands together. "The Sluath took the bodies of these females from their graves, replaced with the bones of another, and brought them back to the underworld, where they returned to life."

Galan's dark face paled. "Culvar."

"Aye. Culvar brought your Fiana back to life, and–" Lilias cried out as Iolar's claws ripped across her breasts and belly. She tottered forward, wrapping her arms around her bleeding torso as she fell to her knees. "And he gave her to the Sluath king for his pleasure."

Galan flung a bolt of power at the prince, knocking him into a tree, and then dropped down to look into Lilias's eyes. "You're Fiana's daughter. 'Tis why you resemble her."

As Iolar rushed at Galan, Danar seized hold of the prince. "You cannot, Prince. He's too powerful."

"I'm the image of my *máthair*," Lilias said and managed to smile. "You should ken that Fiana gave birth to two bairns in the underworld. One she gave to the king. When she saw how cruel her son became, her second bairn she concealed and kept hidden."

"Treasure," the big demon said as he clamped his arms around the prince. "Say no more, or you will die."

She had to speak loudly to be heard over Iolar, who now screamed obscenities at her. "You ken," she yelled, "that the prince murdered our sire to take the throne."

In a blur, Danar threw a blade at her that buried itself in her breast, sending her to her knees.

The terrible wound pumped dark red blood to mix with the rain saturating the ground. But the blade was bronze, not iron, and she might survive it.

Breathing through the pain, Lilias gave Galan her last secret. "After the king died, Iolar then killed his favorite breeder, our *máthair*, Fiana. Your mate."

None of the demons moved, and for a long moment the only sounds came from the storm. Galan looked oddly confused as he slowly turned toward the prince.

Iolar held up his claws in a gesture of surrender.

"I never knew her to be anything but a breeder, Aedth," he said in a shaking voice. "The king never used her name. When he told me that he had bred me on her, I knew then he had to die." He looked around him as if expecting the other demons to agree. "How could I rule the Sluath when anyone might discover my mother was a mortal, and I, a halfling?"

Madness and magic swept through the air as Galan's eyes went completely black.

"You might have been my son." He uttered a stuttering laugh. "My seed killed her, and then *your father's* seed killed her again. He took her from me, and then *you* took her from me." His body seemed to swell with power. *"You facking took her from me."*

Lilias saw him lunge at the prince before an enormous blast heaved her through the air and into the storm.

***

Kiaran fought against Culvar's grip, but only when they dropped down in the tunnel below the pasture did he release him.

"You cannot fight them alone, you fool," the halfling snarled. He jabbed a claw at some descending steps. "Go down two passages and climb the stairs on the left. That will take you out of their sight, where you may signal the others." When he didn't move Culvar shoved him away. "Or return to her now, and you both die."

As the halfling hobbled in the opposite direction, Kiaran made his choice, and ran toward the steps. With every stride he could feel the pain in his wing diminishing, and his body growing stronger. He reached out to his kestrels, and through them saw they had retreated to patrol over the stronghold. He connected his thoughts to Dive's mind, which seemed oddly clouded, and commanded her to find Domnall and the other hunters.

Climbing the stairs out of the passage, Kiaran reached a hatch made of wood. As he lifted it, rain water poured through. He looked out to see the demons on the far side of the pasture. All had clustered around two struggling figures, and ducked and dodged the huge swaths of power being flung in every direction. After a moment he realized Iolar and Galan were now fighting each other. Of Lilias he saw no sign at first, and then he noticed something huddled against the base of a gnarled oak.

He hoisted himself out of the hatch, and kept

low as he hurried across the pasture toward the stronghold. When he stretched out his injured wing it felt almost whole, and with a few more steps he was able to launch himself up from the ground. He gritted his teeth against a fresh wave of pain that slowly dulled as he flew over the stables. On the other side he met his raptors leading the Mag Raith through the rain-soaked wind toward him. He couldn't see Dive, but knew she had to be close.

"They've taken Lilias," he told the other hunters. "She's fallen and likely hurt. Galan has turned on the demon prince. The horde, 'tis in disarray. If we're to lead them to the gate, 'tis now or never."

Domnall nodded. "You see to your lady, and we'll lure the demons into the tunnels."

"Galan wants Lilias," he told the chieftain. "Once I've taken her back, they shall chase after us. You must come behind and assure none escape from the keepe alive."

""Tis too much," Broden muttered. "You bleed, Brother."

"Aye, and the smell shall inflame them even more," Kiaran assured him. "Hide yourselves in the trees. Keep watch, for 'twill be quick."

He left the hunters and soared up into the clouds, beating the currents with his wings until the storm clouds formed a dark gray mass beneath him. Turning to the west, he flew in the direction of the spot where he had seen Lilias, dropping down until he skimmed through the very bottom of the tempest. Through the rain he finally spied the oak, beneath which she lay on her side, one arm flung out, and her cloaking image gone. She looked like a crushed flower, deep rending wounds slashed across her breasts, her wings twisted beneath her.

He forced back his rage as he hovered and watched the demons until he saw his chance. Then he plunged down out of the cloud, scooping up Lilias in his arms.

"You shallnae have her, you bastarts," Kiaran shouted. "She's mine, as she's been since the moment I first put my hands on her." He grinned at Galan, whose face twisted into a snarl of hatred. "And you never shall, you evil fack."

Flying as fast as he could, Kiaran swept over the demons and then headed for the front of the stronghold, keeping Lilias pressed against his chest. He could feel the sluggish beat of her heart, and felt her breath against his neck. That gave him hope as nothing else could.

"You did," she murmured. "Make me. Yours. Love you."

"You shall love me forever," he told her as he dropped down at the entrance to the castle, and ran with her inside. "'Tis no' long enough, but I'll make do." There he waited until he heard the rush of wings drawing closer. "We're going into your brother's lair now. Mayhap he'll give us his blessing."

Kiaran carried her through the diverted passages to the tower where Culvar had uncovered one of the entrances. Carefully he climbed down into the tunnel with her, and rushed toward the lantern Mariena had left burning beside the open gate. It shimmered with magic as soon as he drew near, but so did the opposite wall. An arch appeared in the stone, through which Culvar stepped.

Lilias's lashes fluttered and she sighed before her body went limp.

"My lady?" Kiaran felt all the emotion drain out of him as he touched her cold cheek. "Come now, 'tis no time for such. The horde shall be upon us any moment." He looked up at Culvar, desperate now. "Please. I cannot live without her. Change her skinwork. Restore her life. Bring her back to me."

"I vowed I wouldnae." The halfling reached out and took both her hands, stroking his claws over her fingers. "I shall await my brethren, and see to it they enter the gate. Go with her through the arch. It will take you into the great hall."

Kiaran stared down at his lover's still face.

"Kiaran," Culvar said quietly.

He looked up into the halfling's golden eyes, so like those of Lilias. For a moment, he saw her there, and then she faded. "Aye," he whispered in a tight throat.

Walking through the arch took only a moment, and just as the halfling had promised, they emerged from the wall by the hearth. There Kiaran lay his lady on the fur before the flames, and stretched out beside her.

One by one his kestrels flew into the hall and perched on the floor around him, their feathers soaked, their bright eyes fixed on Lilias. Then Dive fluttered down from Domnall's chair where she had been perching. She came between her master and the body of his beloved, and nestled against his neck to rub her head against his chin.

Only when the kestrel went utterly still did he look down to see the terrible burn on her breast. She had been lightning-struck during the battle, likely trying to protect him the moment he'd been wounded.

As he cradled the dead bird against his heart, Kiaran's thoughts went back through all the centuries to the day he'd met his first little love. He had been gathering berries when he saw the flutter of feathers in the bramble patch. The kestrel clutched a small vole in her claws, but her wings had become snagged on the sharp thorns. The little bird's dark eyes had met his, and she'd stilled. He'd freed her as gently as he could, and then placed her on the ground.

Just as he had done with Lilias, the morning he'd found her in the meadow.

Dive had not lingered. She'd looked up at Kiaran before flying off, and yet returned a short time later, hovering over him.

Holding out his arm, Kiaran had hardly dared to breathe. When the kestrel landed on his wrist, her claws had stabbed deep into his flesh. But he'd been so enchanted by her that he hardly felt the wounds.

In time he'd discovered her nest, buried in a

hollow tree. He brought voles for her and her four young, and wore a leather gauntlet for her to perch on. Soon Dive began teaching her nestlings how to hunt, and Kiaran began to learn, too.

His raptors had been his own little clan, just as Lilias had claimed. But as much as he loved them, he'd long ago resolved to let them go. Had they desired their freedom. Had they ever died.

He closed his eyes, and felt tears streaming down his face.

Lilias and Dive would never come back, but his family awaited. His tribe, the one that Taye had long ago promised him he'd know.

This tribe he would not lose.

Kiaran touched his lips to the kestrel's head, and his lady's brow. Gently he tucked Dive in Lilias's arms before he draped them with his tartan and slowly rose to his feet. His wings flared out as he turned away and headed for the passages.

Chapter Thirty-Four

DOMNALL WATCHED FROM the trees as the Sluath chased after Kiaran, and signaled his hunters to prepare to attack. Seeing Galan leading the pursuit made the anger inside him burn hotter, but he would not abandon reason simply to enjoy defeating a single enemy.

If their plan worked, and Culvar kept his promises, the druid would soon endure suffering of such length and intensity that the chieftain almost felt sorry for him—almost. Galan had been a headman, a leader, a man of faith. What he'd done to betray his responsibilities in his pursuit of his wonts offended Domnall on every level of his being.

Perhaps, he thought, because he might have easily followed the same twisted path.

Broden leaned over to get a better look through the branches. "'Tis all of them, Chieftain, save two."

"There." Edane pointed to the largest and now slowest of the demons, who carried Iolar's battered body over his shoulder. "'Twould seem the druid did some of our work for us."

"Wait." Mael craned his neck. "Three go to perch, see there?"

"Our ladies shall deal with them." Domnall's prediction came true a moment later when a small flurry of iron-tipped bolts flew from the window slits in the tower. All three Sluath took hits to the chest and belly, and plunged to the ground.

The big demon hesitated as he looked back at the trio of dying demons, but then turned his gaze to Galan and the others and continued after them.

"Nearly there, nearly," Broden murmured as he slowly drew his sword. He gathered his reins as he watched, and then nodded. *"Now."*

They flew out of the trees behind the Sluath and attacked. Domnall felt the power of the storm flooding through him as he slammed into an ashen-faced demon, sending it careening into Mael, who impaled it on his sword. An arrow sliced through the downpour from Edane's bow and buried itself in the spine of another. When claws swiped at the side of his face the chieftain wheeled around to decapitate a skull-masked Sluath, kicking away its headless body. He brought his blade back to cleave another, stopping short as he saw the red-gold wings, and his falconer's blazing eyes.

"Lilias?" he shouted to him.

Kiaran shook his head before he barreled into another demon from behind and slashed his throat with a dagger.

Wings and rain and swaths of black blood filled the air as the Mag Raith fought the horde, driving them closer and closer to the front of the stronghold. Broden patrolled from above, assuring none were able to fly up into the storm and get away. The falconer's kestrels joined the battle, their tiny claws ripping at the eyes of the Sluath to blind them. Sand and thorns exploded in the face of every demon who dared stray too near the tower. One by one they fell with crossbow bolts protruding from their smoking bodies.

At the back of the horde Domnall saw Galan, his dark face glowering as he flung bolts of magic at the hunters. One struck Edane, whose body writhed within the dark blue spell for a moment as he closed his eyes. White shimmering magic pierced the shroud around him and peeled it away. Edane made a savage gesture, which threw the remnants of magic at a demon swooping down at him. The Sluath's body exploded in a cloud of ashen black.

A dozen more bodies dropped to curl and wither in the mud. The demons turned en masse and flew into the open entry to the castle. At once Broden descended and fell into line with Domnall and the others as they went to ground. They dismounted together and advanced on the entry. So did the dozens of iron warriors that emerged from the trees.

"Nothing leaves alive," the chieftain told his hunters as the iron warriors marched into Dun Chaill. As soon as the last was within, Domnall led his men in after them. Stone creaked and scraped as Broden used his power to roll a huge boulder behind them, blocking the only way out.

DEEP beneath the glory he had created and called Dun Chaill, Culvar looked at the dark red blood on his claws, and the pale flesh where his Sluath ink had once been. It seemed curious to him that for all the centuries she had spent trapped in the underworld, his sister's blood had never turned black. Lilias had somehow held onto her mortal nature as he never could. How bitter it was to think he might have done the same, had he been born to Fiana instead of his screaming, horrified mother.

Glancing down at his ruined leg, he wondered why he rarely thought of that unfortunate Pritani female. Unlike Fiana she had been taken alive, or so Iolar had once taunted him. Had things been only a little different, Cul might have lived here, in her world, as a full-blood mortal. Even with a much shorter life among her tribe, he likely would have been a happy man. He might have taken a wife, had children of his own, and called men like the Mag Raith his friends.

The Sluath had stolen more than Cul's mother and freedom. They had taken from him the possibility of another, better, cleaner life.

"Forgive me, my lady," Cul said softly to the memory of that long-lost, nameless Pritani slave.

So much of his life had been filled with pain and hatred and vengeance, but Lilias had returned to him all the years she had showered him with joy and light and love. Fiana's kindness and trust, too, for she had treated him not as a monster, but as a son. He remembered the pleasure of having a small, secret family of his own to love and protect. The return of his memories had proven a gift beyond all imagining.

Tonight, he would make amends for all he had done to dishonor Fiana and Lilias. In doing so, he would also pay long overdue tribute to the woman who had given him life.

The sound of wings beating in the passages above drew him from his thoughts, and Culvar opened another portal just beside the gate to the underworld. Limping into it, he stopped on the threshold and covered himself with just enough stone to mask his presence. The rest was up to the Mag Raith.

It didn't take long for the hunters and the iron warriors to drive the demons into the tunnels. Their fear of iron and the rebels combined with their weakness from being unable to devour souls had stolen much of their power. The tattered remains of Iolar's horde hurried from the slashing blades pursuing them toward the gate. They stopped in front of it as if in awe.

"My liege," Danar said. He carried the battered body of the prince under his arm and looked back at Galan Aedth. "This gate remains open. We may use it to return to the underworld."

The druid pushed through the clustering demons and peered into the blackness within the portal. "I see naught." He lifted his hands and passed them back and forth. "I feel naught."

"You won't until you get to the other side," the big demon said. "Then you'll step into the glory of your new kingdom." He gestured toward the opening. "This is where the rebels came through when they found the underworld."

"'Tis time to keep your promise to me," Galan told Danar as he gestured for the other Sluath to go through the gate. "Kill Iolar."

The big demon hesitated, and then put down the prince's limp form. He drew a blade from its sheath in his wing harness, revealing the honed iron of its jagged edge.

He gripped the front of the prince's tunic, but then shoved him through the gate before plunging the dagger into his own chest.

Galan bellowed in fury as Danar collapsed

and shriveled, his broad face shrinking around an oddly peaceful smile.

"My liege." The shape-shifting Seabhag, who now resembled an old, crippled mortal, stared down at the big demon for a moment before he tugged at the druid's arm. "We must leave this place. We can return to slaughter them all another day. Please."

"You shall all die on your knees," Galan shouted at the advancing iron warriors, and then seized Seabhag and dragged him into the gate.

Cul stepped out of his portal and hobbled around Danar's remains as he took his position in front of the gate. The spell he murmured wasn't to close the gate, but to summon what he needed to do so. He stretched out his arms, bracing his hands against either side of the portal. The magic that connected it to the underworld burned along his back, tugging at him, inviting him to go home.

This was his home, Cul thought as the iron warriors began to melt. This spot between the two worlds where he had never belonged, deep beneath his beloved Dun Chaill. He smiled as he realized he would never again have to leave it.

This would be his home forever, just as he had always wished.

Kiaran tried to shove his way through the mass of iron warriors blocking the passage, and felt their metal bodies growing hot. Edane yanked him back as the iron figures began to melt into a spreading pool that sluggishly crept toward the open gate that Culvar now blocked with his body.

"What the fack does he?" Broden demanded.

"Hold," Domnall ordered and stepped closer to the last of the warriors. Its iron had melted away to reveal a head of dark brown hair liberally streaked with silver. More and more of the man became revealed as the metal flowed toward the halfling. "By the Gods. Edane."

The archer came forward, halting as he looked at the man's emerging body. He lifted his hands, which glowed briefly before he dropped them.

"He's mortal," Kiaran whispered. He looked at the other Pritani warriors being revealed by the receding iron. "All of them, they're mortals."

The now-flesh warrior turned, blinking slowly as he lifted a huge, inked hand toward his face. He opened eyes that were as vividly blue as a summer sky, and looked back at the Mag Raith with wonder.

"'Tis ye, my lad," he said to Edane, and reached out a trembling hand. "My son lives."

The archer's knees buckled, and Domnall grabbed him. A moment later Edane embraced his father, both men sobbing with joy.

By the time all of the iron had melted away the men, women and children of the Mag Raith tribe stood staring at Domnall and his hunters. Each one had been inked with Sluath glyphs on their hands or arms. No one seemed to know what to say until a querulous voice came from behind Broden.

"'Tis as I vowed to ye," Ewan said as he slowly walked up to the Pritani. "The beast kept his word to us. The lads took their time finding us, of course, but that I couldnae help."

Domnall regarded the shaman. "You brought the tribe here after us?"

"I couldnae keep them back in the settlement, once I told them what Kiaran confided to me before ye left on yer hunt." He grinned. "The lad warned me Nectan had parlayed with the Romans, and meant to see ye sacrificed to their beastly war god. I reckoned we'd abandon the settlement, find ye, and shelter in the ridges. We tracked ye here, but instead found the beast."

"Ewan bargained for our lives," Edane's sire said. "We'd serve Culvar as his warriors until he took his vengeance against the demons."

"And he made us immortal," the shaman put in. "Like ye, lad."

Kiaran looked over at the halfling, and then rushed through the reawakened Mag Raith to the gate. The iron had collected around Culvar's boots, and now crept up his legs, encasing them as it sealed over the opening to the underworld.

"No demon shall ever pass through this gate again," the halfling said, his voice tight as wisps of smoke rose from his burning form. "And since your chieftain had Lilias do her part, none shall ever travel through time again. I will stand sentry for the Mag Raith, for eternity." He coughed up some dark blood. "You'll look after my sister?"

Kiaran thought of Lilias and Dive as he'd left them, and then offered Culvar the only kindness he could. "Always."

The halfling then met Domnall's gaze. "My castle, 'tis yours."

The entire Mag Raith tribe gathered as the last of the iron that had kept them enchanted spread over Culvar, engulfing his distorted body and forming a huge seal over the gate. At last the spell ended, and Kiaran looked into the iron-clad face in the center of the seal.

Lilias's brother smiled back at him.

Chapter Thirty-Five

※

GALAN STUMBLED OUT of the gate and into a long, dark stone tunnel. For a moment he thought Seabhag had deceived him, and then he saw Iolar's body. He seized the former prince by his gray hair and dragged him toward the dim light at the end of the passage, where the demons had clustered.

"Get out of my way," he demanded, and when they parted he stepped into a huge cavern filled with towering white structures and enormous, strange devices, all encased in sparkling ice. Above the frost-clad city a dome stretched, crossed by the jagged remains of a glass bridge.

On either side of it, huge black craters marred the pristine white walls.

The Sluath limped in to gather around him as he beheld his kingdom, but fear filled their faces.

They feared him, Galan decided as he shook Iolar. "Wake up. 'Tis time to crown me king."

The prince's eyes fluttered, and he groaned as he looked up at the broken bridge. "The cloud stream."

"Aye, we shall use your devices to travel back to Dun Chaill." Galan dragged Iolar closer to his face. "There I shall take the castle to serve as my palace in the mortal realm, and put your head on a pike at the gates."

"We can never travel back." A strange-looking, scarred demon came to stand beside him and gazed up at the dome.

The hopelessness in his eyes made Galan feel impatient. "What mean you? You're masters of time."

"The stream is gone," he said in Seabhag's voice. "So are all the slaves. Treasure must have freed them all before she left the underworld. If she were the last to go…" He shook his head.

The diffused light from overhead began to dim as Galan kicked away the prince and strode back into the tunnel. When he reached the end of the passage, he found a huge round of iron blocking the gate. In the center of the seal stood a figure with a crippled leg.

He tried to summon his magic to blast through the iron, but his power had deserted him. He could feel himself growing weaker by the moment, his wings shrinking, his shoulders stooping. It was all he could do to trot back to where the rest of the demons stood huddled around their dying prince.

"Why do we wither and fade?" Galan demanded. "Tell me."

Iolar pushed himself up from the ice. "We feed on fears. Mortal minds empower us, our enchantments, the time stream, the living stone that creates everything here." He uttered a low, pained whimper. "No mortals, no underworld."

Galan dropped onto the prince, taking hold of his wrinkling face and using the last of his strength to dash his dwindling head against the ice. When black blood sprayed in every direction around them he shoved himself up and turned on Seabhag.

Like the others, the scarred demon had shrunk down to the size of a young bairn. His features contracted into a snarl of old wounds and bleak despair. Chunks of ice and rock began to fall from above, smashing into the crumbling structures and useless devices. A huge chunk of stone slammed down on the demons, crushing several beneath its massive weight.

"I shallnae die," Galan shouted at the others, furiously writhing against the forces squeezing his body into a small, twisted lump. "I'm king of the Sluath."

"Yes, and we're immortal." Seabhag looked up as the dome began to crack. "We'll never die, and we'll never escape this place again."

The dome fractured, and the cavern collapsed with a huge roar, burying them all beneath the rubble.

Sometime later Galan awoke, his body crushed by rock and ice so completely he could not move or speak. He had no power, no senses, no schemes. He felt no madness, only pain and emptiness. As he realized he would remain like this for eternity, he howled without sound.

Galan Aedth, God of nothing, King of no place, Ruler of no one.

Trapped forever alone.

Chapter Thirty-Six

LILIAS FOUND HERSELF walking through a meadow filled with flowers, surrounded by an endless grove of oak trees. Above her the sky stretched black yet clear around an enormous moon and countless stars. The warm air ruffled through the feathers of her wings, and when she looked down at herself she saw no wounds or blood, only a gown of red-gold.

It appeared much like the mortal realm, this starry grove, but she sensed it stood apart from that lovely world.

Two red-haired women stood watching her from the other side of the meadow. One she recognized as Fiana, whose beautiful face lit up with pleasure as their gazes met. The other lady, slender and graceful in her simple shift of white, had Kiaran's smile.

Taye. She wanted to rush toward them, but confusion held her back. If she were here with her mother, and Kiaran's, that meant…

"'Tis over, then?"

A third figure came out of the trees. He stood tall and strong, a Pritani warrior with a handsome face, muscular body, and, Lilias realized, Culvar's features.

"Aye, Sister," he said, his voice deep and strong. "The clan and I trapped the last of the Sluath in the underworld. Never again shall they raid the mortal realm." He gazed at Fiana. "And I made amends to my ladies."

Lilias looked around at the grove, which suddenly felt more ominous. "Must I remain here?"

"'Tisnae a place for ye," Taye said. "No' with your heart, lass."

Fiana walked across the meadow, stopping only a few steps away from Lilias. "Ye must decide yer fate now, Daughter, for you were never mortal. The Gods give ye the right to choose. Come to yer family here, or return to those who await you at Dun Chaill."

"Go to them," Culvar called to her, "and see to it they do not ruin my facking castle."

Taye frowned. "I thought 'twas already a ruin."

Although Lilias smiled a little, and felt reassured, how could she choose? The thought of Kiaran alone in the mortal realm made sorrow well up inside her. Her mother and brother had each other. Her love had his clan.

Then she looked at Taye, and thought of the little lad she had left behind so long ago. In some ways Kiaran would always be that stranded child, just as Lilias would be, yet they had found each other. She had kept him from becoming a demon. He had brought her heart back to life.

Love had saved them both.

In that moment she knew she had no choice at all, really. Still, she had to ask, "You'll wait for me?"

Her mother nodded. "We'll return when 'tis yer time."

Taye came to them, and handed her a small bundle. "To take with you," she said, her dark blue eyes bright with tears. "Tell my lad 'tis a gift from me, as ever 'twas."

When Lilias took the warm bundle Fiana

reached out and touched her hands. Both were marked with black glyphs that turned silver, and then golden. She looked over at her brother, who smiled and nodded.

Lilias would take back another gift of love.

The starry night sky descended, wrapping its soft warmth around her like Kiaran's tartan. The last thing she felt was her mother's kiss on her brow.

※

As Domnall led the hunters, the old shaman, and their reawakened tribe from the tunnels, Kiaran went directly into the great hall. While the Mag Raith celebrated their victory, he would take Lilias and Dive to his tower, and prepare them for burial. He could think of no finer resting place for his kestrel than in the arms of his lady. Yet as he stood over her draped body he found he could not think, much less act.

Lilias had taught him how to feel again, how to love, and how to fight the darkness that had shadowed him since childhood. How would he live without her now?

"Brother." Broden came to stand beside him. "Permit me help you see to her."

Kiaran nodded, and knelt down to gather Lilias's body in his arms. Something twitched under his tartan, bobbing up and down like a small ball before creeping to the edge. A short, curved beak protruded, and then Dive looked up at him through a rent in the plaid, her dark eye filled with exasperation.

"I felt you die." Gently he freed her from the fabric and placed her to perch on his wrist. She ruffled her feathers and puffed out her unmarked breast before uttering a low trill at Lilias. Kiaran glanced down to see his lover's pale face slowly flush with color, and forgot to breathe as he saw her breasts rise and fall with a breath.

"Give me that wee screecher," the trapper said, and gingerly took Dive from him. As the kestrel made scolding sounds he sighed. "Aye, I'm no' your master, but remember I ever trap voles for you and yours, and ask naught in return."

Kiaran hardly heard them for the rushing in his ears. He took Lilias's shockingly warm fingers in his clammy, trembling hands, and saw that the ink marking them had become gilded. Her other hand now bore markings, too, that did the same, making her appear as if she wore gloves of golden lace.

He recalled how Culvar had touched her hands in the tunnel. "My lady?"

Her lashes flickered, and then she awoke with the drowsy expression of one who had overslept. "My love."

As she clasped his hand tighter he felt a surge of power sweep up his arm, and then his skinwork burning as the black ink paled and took on the same gleaming gold color as hers.

Gently Kiaran lifted her from the fur, and held her in his arms as he kissed her lips. She tasted of a moonlit night, and when he looked into her eyes again he saw bits of deep, jeweled blue in the golden bronze irises.

"I let you go," he murmured, looking all over her lovely face.

"Aye." Her lips curved. "I saw Fiana and Culvar, and Taye, I think." Her brow furrowed. "She sent something back with me. She said 'twas her gift to you, as ever 'twas."

"By the Gods." He looked up at Dive, who was busy preening herself. "I've forgotten for so long. Taye loved birds." He touched her hands. "Your skinwork?"

"Culvar gave me his, so that I might come back to you," she said, gazing sadly at her hands.

"'Twas a gift of love," Kiaran told her.

As he helped her to her feet, Domnall, the other hunters and the tribesmen came into the hall. Jenna appeared with Nellie, Mariena and Rosealise, who looked dumbfounded as the chieftain named them. The Pritani embraced each woman as Ewan began introducing the members of the tribe.

"Ye're a wee beauty," Edane's father said to Nellie. "Keep ye my lad on his toes, I reckon."

The American grinned and winked at him. "Dinnae ye ken that, Pops."

"The love my brothers found with their ladies in the underworld," Kiaran said, suddenly understanding. "'Twas what kept them from becoming demons, just as your love saved me."

"Love cannae be enslaved," Lilias said, "or tormented, or taken. 'Tis what makes all hearts immortal. 'Twas the true treasure Iolar and his horde could never find." Lilias slipped her arms around his waist. "Love, 'tis what saves us all, *m'anam*."

As Rosealise and a dozen Pritani women retreated into the kitchens to prepare a massive meal, Domnall sent his hunters to retrieve as many chairs and tables as they could find for the hall.

"We've blankets and linens to cover fleeces on the floors for sleeping tonight," Mael told him. "As for shelter, we've enough rooms for most if they share. Some may have to keep to the barn or the stables until we rebuild more of the towers. We'll need to expand the keepe." He sighed. "By the Gods. In one moment, we go from a clan of ten to a tribe of two hundred and more."

Domnall saw Edane's sire and other men of the tribe approaching him. "Go and help your lady, Seneschal. I'll manage here."

The Mag Raith men greeted him with low, respectful voices, but the seriousness in their eyes boded nothing good.

"We've an old matter to settle, lad," Ewan said as he joined them.

"I freely admit that I ended Nectan the night before we left the tribe." Domnall described the attack in darkness that had led to him killing his sire as he removed his sword and belt.

Jenna came and stood beside him. "Now, wait

a minute. All this happened a thousand years ago. It was self-defense. Also, my husband and his brothers just saved the world, and all of you. How about we give my guy a pass on the automatic death sentence?"

"Automatic?" one of the men echoed, mystified.

"She's American," Ewan told him.

"Wife." Domnall pulled her into his arms, and kissed her before he set her aside. He regarded the men of his tribe and nodded. "'Twasnae planned, nor desired, but I took the life of our headman. I ken the punishment. I ever did. I shallnae resist."

The tribesmen frowned at the shaman, who made a rude sound.

"Had ye no' ended yer sire, I'd have stabbed him in his black heart," Ewan said bluntly. "Ye spared me that. And had we no' followed ye lads, we'd have fallen to the Romans. Now we're all immortal and reunited, so who may fathom the will of the Gods?"

Domnall's wife beamed. "There you go. It all worked out."

As the other men nodded and made affirmative sounds, Edane's sire took from the small pouch he wore around his neck a piece of twisted, worked silver, and handed it to the shaman.

"'Tis yers now, Domnall," Ewan said as he placed it in his hands. "If ye've a mind to take what ye never wished."

"I'm sorry," Jenna said, looking disappointed. "All this hoopla for a pretty old pin?"

"'Tisnae a pin, my love." He took the headman's emblem, made of a circle with three interlocking arcs. "Should I accept, I become headman of the Mag Raith tribe."

"Oh." His wife's expression brightened. "Will that make me headwoman?"

"Would you give me a moment with my lady?" Domnall asked Ewan, who nodded and herded off the tribesmen.

Taking Jenna's hand, the chieftain led her out of the stronghold and out to the curtain wall.

"So, husband," Jenna said, once they were alone. "There's still one thing I don't understand. Just what exactly did Lilias do in the underworld to prevent the Sluath from using the time stream?"

He looked deeply into her violet-blue eyes. "The princess kept her vow to me. She 'twas last to leave." Jenna's jaw dropped a little. "Aye. She released all the slaves. The Sluath returned to emptiness."

"Whoa," she muttered, and looked back at the castle. "She's put 'best friends forever' into a whole new ballpark."

He turned to behold Dun Chaill as well. The storm had left everything soaked, but the clouds had vanished and moonlight silvered every stone, tree, and leaf. In the puddle at his feet the stars twinkled, and the air smelled so clean and fresh it made his lungs tingle with each breath.

"It's beautiful," his wife said, leaning against him.

"'Tis more than that," Domnall said softly. "In there we've two hundred and more Pritani kept enchanted for a hundred centuries. Four ladies from the future who now maynae return. Two half-demons with wings. And we're immortal, all of us, even the kestrels. We're to live in a crumbling castle filled with immortal-killing traps of magic and mayhem we've yet to discover." He gazed into her eyes. "'Tis too much?"

She thought for a moment. "Your tribe seems very nice, and they'll adjust. None of us want to go back to our times, by the way, especially Mariena." She shuddered. "Also, we like our half-demons. Culvar's gone, but we'll deal with the traps. And, now that I have two hundred and more extra hands, I'll rebuild the damn castle."

Domnall smiled. "Naught stops you, my love."

"Naught so far." She smiled up at him. "On a personal note, I think I'd make a fabulous headwoman."

He took her into his arms. "So you shall."

Sneak Peek

Mistress of Misfortune (Dredthorne Hall Book 1)

Excerpt

CHAPTER ONE

DRIVING TO DREDTHORNE Hall had not been Miss Meredith Starling's original intention when she had set out from the house that afternoon. In the rig she carried two baskets of fine, ripe apricots to be delivered to the village, along with messages from her mother.

"Tell the sisters Brexley these should do very well for jam," Lady Helena Starling had said from the morning room chaise lounge she occupied most of each day. "But they must use them before Sunday or they will surely go rotten. Pray do not put the second basket into the vicar's hands, for I know Mr. Branwen will eat too many and make himself sick again. You may take them to his wife directly, for she will know where to best conceal them until she can make them into tarts. You are certain that you do not wish Percival to accompany you?"

"I am, Mama." Meredith smiled to conceal her annoyance. "Now rest, and I will be back in time for tea."

As she drove from her parent's modest estate Meredith still brooded over the necessity to insist she could manage the simple errand alone. Her mother often begged Captain Percival Starling to play her escort, something that mortified Meredith. She was very fond of her cousin, but she certainly didn't require him to tag along after her everywhere. Meredith had already made peace with the misfortune that plagued her life; why couldn't her mother?

Agitation kindled a rare flash of rebellion, and when Meredith reached the crossroads she turned the rig in the opposite direction from the village. She needed more time to sort out her thoughts before she braced the vicar and the Sisters Brexley. Surely it would do no harm to enjoy the crisp air and golden sunlight by herself; anyone would agree that it was the perfect day for a ride through the country.

You mean another ride past The House, her conscience chided.

Meredith would never admit it to another soul, but long ago she had formed a secret fascination for Dredthorne Hall. Built over a century past by Emerson Thorne, an immensely wealthy gentleman with a scandalous affection for French chateaus, the old house stood like a brooding bastion of hauteur on a high hill overlooking the sprawling lands and forests belonging to the estate. Compared to the other country manors neighboring the village it seemed wholly out of place. Yet while many disdained Dredthorne's elegantly shabby facade, unfashionable staircase towers and overgrown terraced gardens, Meredith had always felt a strange affinity with the house.

No other young ladies of her acquaintance shared her interest, but that had more to do with the Thorne family curse.

The dark, wicked legends about Dredthorne Hall abounded, of course. Like all small villages,

Renwick had stalwart gossips who collected such scandalous lore to discuss in avid murmurs over afternoon tea. Some insisted that the original owner had died of a broken heart on the very day the house was finished (Meredith's father claimed that tale a ridiculous fiction, as church records plainly showed Mr. Thorne had occupied the house for over a decade before succumbing to a prolonged illness.) Several servants who had abruptly left their positions at the estate claimed ghosts wandered wailing through the halls at night (Meredith's mother insisted this was petty revenge on their part for being dismissed for various infractions.) Even more fantastic tales of Dredthorne's lost treasures and ferocious monsters frequently circulated, all of which came without a mention of witnesses or a shred of proof.

The most persistent and ominous rumor had always been the Thorne family curse. According to the local tell-tales, every master of Dredthorne was doomed to fall in love with a lady who spent a night in the house. This then cursed not the gentleman but the lady, for anyone who dared to become the mistress of Dredthorne Hall inevitably came to a swift, horrible end.

"Some go mad and must be locked away, poor dears," Meredith's aunt insisted. "Others vanish, never to be seen again. But most of the poor ladies are found dead in that wretched house, always within a few months of the wedding. Slain by their evil husbands, I daresay."

While every gossip in the village repeated this nonsense as absolute fact, Meredith found it almost laughable. The masters of Dredthorne had likely been no more cursed or evil than any fabulously wealthy gentlemen. She felt sure such privileged Londoners viewed the country as a place of respite, not residence.

No Thorne had even bothered to visit Dredthorne Hall for the last fifty years, until the new heir had arrived a month past.

As for that mysterious gentleman being cursed to love only a woman who spent the night alone in his house, to Meredith that seemed an utter Banbury tale. He certainly would be obliged to marry such a lady—but only if he wished to avoid ruining her reputation and permanently incurring the wrath of her family. She imagined honor-bound marriages did take place regularly in London, where society was fast, immense, and said to thrive on such intrigues, but they simply didn't happen here.

In Renwick the modest social calendar moved at a crawl. Every family knew each other, and closely watched over every unmarried daughter until her most advantageous match could be arranged. Indeed, a young lady could not wear a new bonnet to church without becoming the talk of the villlage.

"Not that I'll ever marry, Bessie," Meredith told her horse as she tugged on the reins to slow the rig. "Perhaps if I remind Mama of that, she will not mind so much letting me out of our house."

Bessie's bridle jingled as she shook her head and snorted.

As her elderly parents' primary source of companionship Meredith devoted much of her time to them. Being a good and attentive daughter was the only way she could show her gratitude for the endless trouble her misfortunes had caused them. Yet as the years passed, and all of her friends married and started their families, her own loneliness grew.

Unhappily that, like Meredith's luck, would never change.

Ahead of the rig the road smoothed out and forked off into the first of the four drives traversing the grounds of Dredthorne Hall. On each side of the long-bricked drive twin stately lions carved from moss-mottled Italian marble sat atop Doric-styled pedestal columns to which iron gates had once been attached. They had likely been removed some time in the past by a tenant seeking more ready access to the estate, and since never replaced.

"Good morning, Augustus, Tiberius," Meredith murmured, ducking her head in mock deference as she passed them. As a girl she'd been a little afraid of the fierce-faced beasts, for it had seemed as if they had glared directly down at her. Once she had secretly named them, however, they seemed far less imposing.

She then looked up at The House (for Meredith could not think of it as anything less grand); which sat like an aging beauty in her best finery atop that immaculate hill, waiting for a beau that would never come.

A veteran of many such rides, Bessie slowed on her own while Meredith beheld Dredthorne's expansive north facade. Soft grey slate roofs capped the mellow buff stone and brick of the house, which flanked by its unusual staircase towers on either end presented to the eye like a small castle. Constructed of towering, intricately-sculpted marble panels depicting life-sized warrior angels, the front vestibule had an unearthly quality more like a gateway to another world than an entrance to a dwelling. Sadly, time had weathered the exterior, adding cracks and pitting to nearly all of the house's features, but for Meredith that added to its air of mystery. In the sunlight the house took on a faint glow that obscured most of the obvious decay, making it shimmer against the horizon.

How could anyone believe such a lovely place to be dark or wicked?

Meredith tugged Bessie to a stop, and regarded the house for a long moment before she allowed herself a single, unhappy sigh. She would have given anything to see the inside, but her parents were hardly sociable. She could not recall the last time they had gone out to call on their neighbors; they preferred to host friends at their home. Aside from seeing to the occasional errand, and attending church services on Sunday, Meredith also rarely went anywhere. That was not likely to change, either, thanks to

Dredthorne's new master, the reclusive Colonel Alistair Thorne.

The ladies of the village had much to say about the colonel, as they had grown seriously displeased with him.

"We were so looking forward to welcoming the colonel into our society," Lady Hardiwick had told Meredith's mother when she came with several of her friends for tea. "But he will not have us. He accepts none of our invitations, and has his man turn away every caller at the door."

"Perhaps he is ill, my lady, and cannot stand the company as yet," the vicar's wife, Mrs. Branwen, suggested with her usual cautious diffidence. "Mr. Branwen mentioned that he is just returned from serving in India."

Her ladyship sniffed. "Our dear Gerald is come back to us this very month on injury leave, with his bad leg still paining him terribly. Yet compared to the colonel, my son is the toast of the town."

"Thorne is likely still occupied with settling his domestics," Meredith's mother said, and then frowned. "Do you know, I have heard that he brought them with him from India. All of them men."

"Heathens in turbans, I was told," Lady Hardiwick said, her expression darkening. "They speak no English and dress very oddly. I think it disgusting."

"Surely not," Mrs. Branwen said. "It is an act of charity to bring them here, and give them work."

"That is his problem," Lady Starling told her. "A single man can never manage a household with any degree of competence, and he has the added misfortune of overrunning his with foreigners. No wonder he cannot get on. I wager he will very soon be of a mind to be more sociable, if only to find a wife."

"Well, he will not have my Prudence," Lady Hardiwick stated flatly. "I don't care how rich he is, you know what they say about ladies who marry Thorne men. And I refuse to have such a strange, disagreeable fellow as my son-in-law."

Meredith recalled how tightly she had pressed her lips together after that remark. Prudence Hardiwick was five years her senior, and while passably attractive had no personality. Whenever a man spoke to her, she giggled incessantly, a habit she had cultivated sometime during her three seasons in London. No gentleman had ever offered for her, much to no one's surprise and her mother's great displeasure.

These days Prudence spent most of her time in the company of her friends as they shopped, gossiped and ogled any member of the militia unfortunate enough to cross their path. No doubt being presented to Colonel Thorne would send Prudence into mirthful paroxysms, but Meredith imagined the simpering lady would have little appeal for such a traveled veteran.

"I expect I have now dashed your hopes, Meredith," Lady Hardiwick said, and patted her hand. "But you are the better for it. No young lady should saddle herself with an unmannerly husband, no matter how desperate her situation."

"Indeed." Meredith smiled as she imagined pouring the rest of her tea over her ladyship's feathered bonnet. "You are very kind to say so, ma'am."

"My poor darling girl." Lady Starling released a long sigh. "Her father and I cannot work out why she must suffer so terribly, for she is everything sweetness," she said, as if her daughter wasn't in the room.

"I am not suffering, Mama," Meredith said quietly. "I always mend."

Lady Starling ignored her to address the vicar's wife. "I live for the day that the good Lord hears my prayers, Deidre, and removes this terrible burden from her."

"I am sure He will, my lady." Mrs. Branwen gave Meredith a sympathetic look. "You seem quite recovered from that dreadful fall you had last month, my dear."

Meredith forced a smile. "I am, ma'am, thank you."

Now, sitting outside Dredthorne, Meredith could understand why the colonel had refused to have anything to do with his neighbors. Country villages were filled with the hopeful and often conniving parents of unmarried daughters; he must have known he'd be a target of matrimonial machinations from the moment he moved into the house. Still, it was odd that he had refused to allow *any* callers. The vicar would have been among the first to attempt to welcome him, and no one ever turned away the perennially ebullient Mr. Branwen.

Perhaps he is too unwell to accept visitors. Whenever Meredith's bad luck resulted in an injury she wanted to do nothing but stay in her room and be left alone until the pain eased. A soldier like the colonel would understand how difficult it was to put on a brave face when one felt–

"Out of the way!"

The shout wrenched Meredith from her thoughts, and she glanced over her shoulder to see a farmer with a heavily-laden cart barreling straight at her. Quickly she slapped Bessie's rump with the reins, and drove the rig to one side to allow him past. As soon as he did, Bessie whinnied angrily and started off after him.

"Whoa, girl, whoa," Meredith called out, tugging desperately on the reins.

• • • • •

Buy *Mistress of Misfortune (Dredthorne Hall Book 1)*

Glossary

Here are some brief definitions to help you navigate the medieval world of the Clan Mag Raith series, and also Mariena's French and German below.

Clan Mag Raith

alpha: lead or dominant
a thasgaidh: Scots Gaelic for "my darling"
amaro: a bittersweet herbal liqueur blended with gin and vermouth to make a Hanky-Panky cocktail
aquila: Latin for "eagle", the standard of a Roman legion
aulden: medieval slang for "archaic"

bairn: child

Banbury tale: Victorian slang for a nonsensical story

bannock: a round, flat loaf of unleavened Scottish bread

bloodwort: alternate name for yarrow

bloomers: Victorian word for "trousers"

blue-stocking: Victorian slang for "intellectual"

boak: Scottish slang for "vomit"

borage: alternate name for starflower (*Borago officinalis*)

broch: an ancient round hollow-walled structure found only in Scotland

burraidh: Scots Gaelic for "bully"

cac: Scots gaelic for "shit"

cat's pajamas: Roaring Twenties slang for something wonderful

chain hoist: tackle and chain device used to lift heavy objects

chanter: a woodwind instrument used alone as practice for playing the bagpipes

charnel pit: a vault where human remains are stored

chebs: Scottish slang for "breasts"

conclave: druid ruling body

coopered: Victorian slang for worn out

Cornovii: name by which two, or three, tribes were known in Roman Britain

cossetted: cared for in an overindulgent way

cottar: an agricultural worker or tenant given lodgings in return for work

Cuingealach: Scots Gaelic for "the narrow pass"

curate: a member of the clergy engaged as an assistant to a vicar, rector, or parish priest

deadfall trap: a type of trap fashioned to drop a heavy weight on the prey

deamhan (plural: *deamhanan*): Scots Gaelic for demon

dolabra: Latin for "pickaxe"

don't take any wooden nickels: early 20th century American slang for "don't do something stupid"

doss: leaves, moss, and other detritus covering the ground dru-wid: Proto Celtic word; an early form of "druid"

drystane: a construction of stacked stone or rock that is not mortared together

dunnage: Victorian slang for "clothing"

fash: feel upset or worried

fizzing: Victorian slang for "first-rate" or "excellent"

fletching: feathering an arrow

flight: a group of kestrels

floorer: Victorian slang for "knocking someone down"

flummery: a custard-like Welsh dessert made from milk, beaten eggs and fruit

footman: a liveried servant whose duties include admitting visitors and waiting at table

forthright: honest

fortitude: courage under pressure

frittata: Italian egg dish similar to a crustless quiche

gainsay: contradict

give the sack: English slang for "firing someone from their job"

gladii: Latin plural of *gladius* or "sword"

glock: Victorian slang for "half-wit"

gongoozler: Victorian slang for "an idle, dawdling person"

goof: early 20th century American slang for "a man in love"

grice: a breed of swine found in the Highlands and Islands of Scotland and in Ireland

istrumagi: Norse for "fat gut"

groat: a type of medieval silver coin worth approximately four pence

gu bràth: Scots Gaelic for forever, or until Judgment

Guédelon: a 25-year-long archaeological experiment in Treigny, France to recreate a 13th century castle

hold your wheesht: Scottish slang term for "maintaining silence and calm"

hoor: medieval slang for "whore", "prostitute"

hoosgow: Roaring Twenties slang for jail

Hussar: member of the light cavalry

in the scud: Scottish slang for "naked"

jarl: a Norse chief

jem: Medieval Scots slang for a person prized for beauty and excellence, a "gem"

jess: a short leather strap that is fastened around each leg of a hawk

kirk: Scottish slang for "church"

kithan: Medieval Scots term for a "demon"

knacker: Victorian slang for "an old, useless horse"

laudanum: a tincture of opium

lay about: lazy person

luaidh: Scots Gaelic for "loved one" or "darling"

maister: medieval slang for "master" or "leader"

make a stuffed bird laugh: Victorian slang phrase for something that is "preposterous or contemptible"

make like the canary: Roaring Twenties slang for confess

m'anam: Scots Gaelic for "my soul"

marster: medieval slang for "master"

máthair: Scots Gaelic for "mother"

Mulligatawny soup: a spicy British soup

nag: slang for horse

naught-man: an unearthly creature that only looks like a man

nock: the slotted end of an arrow that holds it in place on the bowstring

Noreg: medieval name for Norway

Odin: the king of the Norse Gods and Asgard, father of Thor

oskilgetinn: Norse for someone born out of wedlock

panay: alternate name for self-heal (*Prunella vulgaris*)

pantaloons: Victorian word for "trousers"

parti: the ideas or plans influencing an architect's design

peignoir: Victorian-era woman's garment similar to a "negligee or a light dressing gown"

peridot: a green semi-precious mineral, a variety of olivine

peyrl: Scots Gaelic for "pearl"

plumbata: lead-weighted throwing dart used by the Romans

pomatum: greasy, waxy, or water-based substance used to style hair

quern: a primitive hand mill for grinding grain made of two stones

rags: Roaring Twenties slang for clothes

rollicking: fun and boisterous

rooing: removing sheep's loose fleece by hand-pulling

sad sap: Roaring Twenties slang for a dumb guy

sham: false, fake

Sheba: Roaring Twenties slang for a woman with sex appeal

sica: a long curved dagger

skeg: Scots Gaelic for "demon"

slant: Roaring Twenties slang for take a look at

sleep-in: Victorian slang for sleeping in late

snuggleup: Roaring Twenties slang for a man who enjoys petting

spend: ejaculate

stand hunt: to watch for prey from a blind or place of concealment

stele: an upright pillar bearing inscriptions

stockman: a person who looks after livestock

strewing: plants scattered on the floor as fragrance, insecticide, and disinfectant taking a bounce: Roaring Twenties slang for to get kicked out

tapachd: Scots Gaelic for "an ability of confident character not to be afraid or easily intimidated"

taverit: Scottish slang for "worn out, exhausted"

tear bottle: Used in the Victorian revival of the ancient custom of catching tears of mourning in a small vial with a loose stopper. When the bottled tears evaporated, the period of mourning was considered over.

thane: one who serves the jarl

Thor: the Norse God of lightning and thunder

torque: a medieval neck ornament

touch-reader: a person with psychometric ability; someone who touch objects to envision their history

trigging: in stonework, using wedge pieces to secure a construct

treadwheel crane: a human-powered wooden wheeled device used for hoisting and lowering materials

trodge: Scottish slang for "trudge"

valise: a small traveling bag or suitcase

woundwort: alternate name for wound healer (*Anthyllis vulneraria*) yelm: bundled block of straw or grasses used in thatching

French to English:

bien sûr: of course
boche: blockhead, a derogatory term used during WWII for Nazi soldiers
bon sang: damn it
bonjour: good morning
bravo: well done
calme-toi: calm down
c'est bon: French for "it's good"
coup d'un soir: one-night stand
désolé: I'm sorry (casual form)
enchanté: nice to meet you
Favor: the name of a WWII-era French bicycle manufacturer
hostilité: hostility
imbécile: imbecile, stupid
je me suis échappé: I escaped
je suis le cygne: I am the swan
je t'aime: I love you
la patronne: the boss
le cygne: the swan
ma chére amie: my dear friend

ma copine: my friend
mademoiselle: French for "Miss"
merde alors: shit then
mon ami: my friend
mon ange: my angel
mon charmant: my charming one
mon couer: my heart
mon cygne: my swan
mon dieu: my god
monsieur: sir
n'aie pas peur: French for ""Don't be afraid"
ne pleure pas: I am not crying
non: French for "no"
*nous sommes tes ami*s: French for "We are your friends"
oui: French for "yes"
putain: whore
resistants: resisters, a slang term for WWII French Resistance agents
reste en arriére: French for "Stay back"
trés bon: very good
vous parlez anglaise: French for "Do you speak English?"

German to English:

fuhrer: leader
Gestapo: secret state police (formally Geheime Staatspolizei)
guten abend, herren: good evening, gentlemen
Hauptsturmführer: Nazi party paramilitary rank, equal to Captain in the German army
Luftwaffe: Air Force

Pronunciation Guide

A selection of the more challenging words in the Immortal Highlander, Clan Mag Raith series. French and German follow below.

a thasgaidh: AH-tas-GEH
Aklen: ACK-lin
aquila: uh-KEE-lah
Bacchanalian: back-NIL-ee-ahn
bannock: BAN-ick
boak: BOWK
Bridget McMurphy: BRIH-jet mick-MER-fee
Broden mag Raith: BRO-din MAG RAYTH
burraidh: BURR-ee
cac: kak

Carac: CARE-ick
Clamhan: CLEM-en
Clarinda Gowdon: kler-IN-dah GOW-don
Cornovii: core-KNOW-vee-eye
Cuingealach: kwin-GILL-ock
Cul: CULL
Danar: dah-NAH
Dapper: DAH-purr
Darro: DAR-oh
deamhan: DEE-man
dolabra: dohl-AH-brah
Domnall mag Raith: DOM-nall MAG RAYTH
Druman: DREW-mawn
Dun Chaill: DOON CHAYLE
Eara: EER-ah
Edane mag Raith: eh-DAYN MAG RAYTH
Ewan: YOO-in
Fargas: FAR-gus
Fiana: FEYE-eh-nah
Fraser: FRAY-zir
Frew: FREE
frittata: free-TAH-tah
Galan Aedth: gal-AHN EEDTH
gladii: GLAHD-ee-ee
groat: GROWT

gu bràth: GOO BRATH
Hal Maxwell: HOWL MACK-swell
Helen Frances Quinn: HELL-uhn FRAN-sess KWIN
Hussar: hoo-ZAHR
Iolar: EYE-el-er
istrumagi: ih-stroo-MAH-gee
Jackie Facelli: JA-kee fah-CHELL-ee
Jaeg: YEGG
jarl: YARL
jem: GEM
Jenna Cameron: JEHN-nah CAM-er-ahn
John McMurphy: JAWN mick-MER-fee
Josef: HOE-zef
Kehl: HEEL
Kiaran mag Raith: KEER-ahn MAG RAYTH
kithan: KEY-tin
laudanum: LAH-deh-num
luaidh: LOO-ee
Lyle Gordon: lie-EL GORE-din
Mael mag Raith: MAIL MAG RAYTH
maister: MAY-ster
m'anam: MAH-nuhm
Marie-Anne: mah-REE-en
Mariena Douet: mah-REE-nah DOO-eh

marster: MAR-stir
Mary Gowdon: MARE-ee GOW-don
máthair: muh-THERE
Meirneal: MEER-nee-el
Michael Patrick Quinn: MYK-uhl PAH-treek KWIN
Mickie: MIH-kee
Mulligatawny: mull-eh-gah-TAWN-ee
Nectan: NECK-tin
Nellie: NELL-ee
Njal: NYULL
Noreg: NORG
Odin: OHTH-in
okilgetinn: oh-skihl-GEH-tin
parti: PAR-tee
peignoir: pen-WAH
peyrl: PEH-rill
plumbata: PLOOM-bah-tah
pomatum: pah-MADE-uhm
quern: KWERN
Rodney Percell: RAHD-knee purr-SELL
Rosealise Dashlock: roh-see-AH-less DASH-lock
Seabhag: SHAH-vock
Serca: SAIR-eh-kah
sica: SEE-kah
Sileas: SIGH-lee-ess

skeg: SKEHG
Sluath: SLEW-ahth
tapachd: TAH-peed
taverit: tah-VAIR-eet
Taye: TEH
thane: THAYN
Thor: TOHR
tisane: TEE-zahn
torque: TORK
trodge: TRAHJ
valise: vuh-LEES
Wachvale: WATCH-veil
wheesht: WEESHT

French words:

bien sûr: BEE-yen SIR
boche: BOSH
bon sang: BOW SAW
bonjour: bah-ZHURE
bravo: BRA-voh
calme-toi: CAL-meh TWAH
coup d'un soir: COO-der SWAH
désolé: DEZ-oh-lay
enchanté: aw-shawn-TAY
hostilité: hoe-STILL-lee-tay

imbécile: eyem-bee-SILL-lay
je me suis échappé: ZHAY MAY SWEE eh-SHAH-pay
je suis le cygne: ZHUH SWEE -LAH-SEEN
je t'aime: zhuh TEM
la patronne: LAH PAH-tren
le cygne: LUH SEEN
Lyon: lee-AWN
ma chére amie: MAH SHER ah-MEE
ma copine: MAH coh-PEEN
merde alors: MARED a-LOR
mon ami: MAWN ah-MEE
mon ange: MAWN ANZH
mon charmant: MAWN shar-MAWN
mon couer: MAWN CUR
mon cygne: MAWN SEEN
mon dieu: MAWN DEW
monsieur: meh-SYOUR
ne pleure pas: NEH PLUR PAH
putain: pooh-TAWN
resistants: ray-ZIS-tawns
trés bon: TRAY BAWN

German words:

fuhrer: FYER-er

Gestapo: gesh-STAH-poh
guten abend, herren: GOO-ten AH-bend HAIR-en
Hauptsturmführer: HAWP-SHTERM-FYER-er
Luftwaffe: LOOFT-wah-fah

Dedication

For Mr. H.

Copyright

Copyright © 2019 Hazel Hunter

This is a work of fiction. Names, characters, places, and incidents are products of the author's imagination or are used fictitiously and are not to be construed as real. Any resemblance to actual events, locales, organizations, or persons, living or dead, is coincidental.

All rights reserved. No part of this book may be used or reproduced in any manner, stored in or introduced into a retrieval system, or transmitted, in any form, or by any means (electronic, mechanical, photocopying, recording, or otherwise), without the prior written consent of the copyright owner.

The scanning, uploading, and distribution of this book via the Internet or via any other means without the permission of the copyright owner is illegal. Please purchase only authorized electronic editions, and do not participate in or encourage electronic piracy of copyrighted materials. Your support of the author's rights is appreciated.